Escape of the Scout
Escape, Book 1
Mary Lancaster

Escape of the Scoundrel

All Rights Reserved © 2025 by Mary Lancaster
No part of this book may be reproduced or transmitted in any form or by any means, graphic, electronic, or mechanical, including photocopying, recording, taping, or by any information storage or retrieval system, without the written permission of the publisher.

Chapter One

Lord Illsworth was in a foul mood.

Not only had he lost far too much money backing the wrong man in the afternoon's prize fight, but he'd got soaking wet driving his curricle back from the fight field to the Duck and Spoon at Cartbridge afterwards. The puny coin he'd lingered at the fight to win from the idiots Dolton and Poole—aptly known as Dolt and Fool—did not make up for either of those disasters.

It all boded ill for being able to recoup his losses through card games at Lady Grandison's party this week. Although, to be sure, there *would* be the welcome distraction of the delectable Lady Bab, who was surely bored with her dull stick of a husband and ripe for the plucking at last. After all, she had given him her token, even if she had asked for it back again almost immediately. There was pleasure—and mischief—to be had there.

Cheered by this thought, he walked, dripping, into the riotous Duck and Spoon Inn. And the first man he saw was Snake Bloody Sanderly.

Not that Snake was likely to attend Lady Grandison's party, let alone defend his sister Bab's honour, but the man was guaranteed to upset the most convivial gathering. Even now, he stood out from among the drunken young bloods and the over-excited sporting Corinthians, simply by *lounging* at his ease at the table next to the staircase. He was dressed with his usual quiet elegance, not a raven lock out of place, the familiar, maddening half-sneer upon his thin lips, one upward-sloping eyebrow raised at young rakehell, Lord Durward, who sat opposite him.

Another enthusiast, Wriggley by name and nature, stood before Sanderly, gesticulating wildly as he explained the fight to him, move by move. Snake's expression was one of undisguised boredom. His eyelids were drooping in what should have been a warning.

Illsworth moved surreptitiously toward the stairs, hoping not to be noticed until he looked more presentable.

Interrupting Wriggley without apology, Sanderly addressed Durward in his soft yet curiously penetrating voice. "Is this fellow talking to you?"

"Can't be," Durward said. "I was there."

Sanderly glanced up at Wriggley who had finally noticed they were talking through him. "So was I."

Wriggley flushed. "Your lordship is a devotee of the science of pugilism?"

"Not devoted to anything, my dear fellow. But I know a man just dying to be lectured. You'll find him..." Sanderly's hood-like eyelids snapped fully up, revealing eyes of an intense, almost inhuman shade of blue as he glanced maliciously around the room in search of a victim.

Illsworth froze, his foot on the first step of the staircase. Inevitably, the blue, world-mocking gaze found him, taking in his dripping person, from his muddy hat—it had blown off in the wind as he rounded a bend in the road—and plastered hair, over the streams of water still running off every cape of his coat, to his squelching boots.

"Dear me," he drawled. "Is it raining?"

Durward let out a crack of laughter. Which drew everyone else's attention and a few grins, some of them sympathetic.

"As you see," Illsworth said shortly. "Obviously, I don't run as fast as you."

He thought this a rather clever riposte, for rumour said the blackguard Earl of Sanderly, cashiered from the army for cowardice, was bolting now from English shores. Opinions varied as to why. Some said he was escaping assassins or angry husbands, others that he was just fed-up being blackballed from the best London clubs. At the very least, Illsworth's remark should have annoyed Sanderly. It certainly won a few malicious laughs.

But the earl only smiled. "Oh, I never run. I have servants and horses for that kind of thing. Best hurry along and change before you catch a chill, Illsworth. Thank you, George." The gratitude was flung at the innkeeper who placed a bottle and one glass at his elbow. Well, no one else would drink with the Snake.

Even this belief, annoyingly, proved to be untrue, for when Illsworth returned in dry coat, pantaloons, and boots, he found several men clustered around the earl's table, setting up a game of hazard among several bottles and glasses.

"Join us, Illsworth?" Lord Wolf invited. He had wagered correctly on the prize fight, but Illsworth saw with predatory pleasure that he had an oddly reckless look in his eyes that boded well for his opponents.

"Why not?" Illsworth said pulling up a chair. He might even get a chance later to make use of his weighted dice and fleece everyone, including Sanderly which would be a special satisfaction.

Wolf drank steadily. So did Sanderly, though it never changed his weary expression. Durward knocked it back with enthusiasm. Illsworth smiled and almost rubbed his hands together. Then he realized Sanderly's heavily lidded eyes were upon him and hastily conjured up a harmless reason for amusement.

"Is this a peers only table?" he inquired, for it did stand out among the chaos in the rest of the room. A few pinks of the ton with quizzing glasses were comparing waistcoats at one end of the room. At another, a convivial fellow was trying to perform a handstand on the table while his friends roared with laughter. Everyone else was milling around, some re-enacting the fight while others argued over every move and interfered to show how it *really* happened.

Illsworth's table companions, who were indeed mostly peers of the realm, accorded his remark a cursory grin, all but Sanderly who appeared to have lost interest. His gaze was on a young gentleman limping painfully across the floor with a stout walking stick, presumably in search of somewhere to sit.

Bad luck, thought Illsworth without real sympathy. The Duck and Spoon was packed to the gunnels for the night with the rich and privileged. This rather ordinary fellow did not stand a chance of a room or even a seat. He had straight, fair hair and deep lines around his eyes and mouth but despite his awkward gait, his posture was very upright. Possibly an injured soldier back from the Peninsula. Or America.

His gaze flickered over the "peers' table" as he passed, and his eyes widened with startled pleasure. He stopped, hobbled nearer, and thrust out his free hand. "Snake!"

This will be good, Illsworth thought with amusement. Sanderly could annihilate encroachers—his definition was satisfyingly wide—and frequently did, with no more than a raised eyebrow or two devastating words. Which was usually vastly entertaining for watchers and humiliating for the encroacher.

But to Illsworth's astonishment, Sanderly actually smiled—not his usual sneer either, but a spontaneous, singularly sweet smile. He even reached up to clasp the proffered hand in what from anyone else would have been a warm shake.

"Jonny Berry, as I live and breathe. Join us? Budge up there, Wolf."

Obligingly, Wolf shuffled along the bench and they made space for the newcomer, who sat down with a grunt of relief and propped his walking stick up against the wall behind him.

"Captain Berry," Sanderly introduced his friend. "Jonny, Lords Durward, Illsworth, and Wolf."

Everyone nodded and murmured wary greetings. After all, the man appeared to be a friend of Snake's. One could almost forget that Sanderly had once been an army officer too, though inevitably he had been cashiered for cheating or cowardice or treason. Or all three.

"And you're a lord yourself, now, I hear," Captain Berry grinned, looking him up and down. "I almost didn't recognize you! Do I congratulate you?"

"No." A plate of beef pie was set before Sanderly who promptly ordered for the captain, too, and demanded another bottle.

After that, things settled down into a more predictable pattern. Captain Berry said little, eating and drinking rather more sparingly than the rest, no doubt overwhelmed by the august company. Occasionally, he cast odd, almost disappointed glances at Sanderly when his lordship deigned to make one of his sarcastic remarks.

"Will you play, Captain?" Wolf invited as they began a fresh game.

"If the stakes are not beyond me," Berry said mildly, which ensured they began rather ludicrously low. Secretly, Illsworth was grateful, for he could not guarantee a large win until later in the evening when he could swap his own dice.

There were distractions, of course. An apparently impromptu cock fight was in full swing at the far end of the room, accompanied by yells of encouragement, demented clucking, rampant wagering and clouds of floating feathers. The maids—extra women had clearly been recruited for the evening—were kept busy, delivering ale and bottles, weaving between clowning crowds and avoiding groping hands and eager laps. A couple of other girls, presumably not employed at the inn, seemed to have come only for the wealthier laps, and their screeches of laughter and feigned shock mingled with the rest of the racket.

A few youths were trying to bet on a snail race, although the creatures kept being crunched underfoot. A small goat had also been introduced into the company, with the purpose of seeing who it would butt first.

At hazard, Illsworth won modestly, even when Sanderly held the bank.

Outside, the stagecoach arrived in a mad flurry of lights and activity. Luggage was thrown down from the coach roof, the blowing horses were unharnessed and a fresh team brought up ready to take their place. A stout woman with a basket alighted, followed by a gaggle of children and a ridiculously pretty girl in a dark traveling cloak and a rather squashed straw bonnet with blue ribbons.

Illsworth sat up. Surely the girl could not belong to the stout matron? He didn't fancy the family's chances if they dared step into the inn! But no, the stout lady sailed away to a waiting gig with her even larger husband. The delectable girl was smiling and herding the children toward the inn's front door.

"Is *she* in for a shock," Illsworth murmured with amusement.

"Bet, my lord," Durward said to him impatiently, eyes glittering with brandy. When had he started on the brandy?

Illsworth made his bet and gazed expectantly at the inn's front door, where two youths were dancing enticingly in front of the goat who seemed to be trying to dodge around them rather than butt either of them. The door opened and the girl sailed in alone.

"Shut the door!" yelled several voices as the goat made a bid for freedom.

The girl shut the door and leaned against it, her eyes widening with clear astonishment.

Her gaze was fixed not on any of the gawping young men who had fallen silent in appreciation of the beauty before them, nor even the blood and feathers of the cockfight across the room, but on the little goat, bleating piteously.

"I *say*," Durward murmured appreciatively.

One of the lap girls seized the dropping jaw of her drunken swain and turned it forcibly back toward her.

The young woman at the door raised outraged eyes to the innkeeper, who was hurrying toward her with some alarm.

"What is that poor creature doing in here?" the girl demanded, her accent unexpectedly refined.

"Butting me," claimed the nearest wagerer proudly.

"It never touched you," disputed his friend. "It's about to butt *me*."

"Its mother will butt you both," the girl said, scowling at the innkeeper. "The poor little thing is terrified. Please take it back to its mother now."

"Of course, miss, of course," the innkeeper said in somewhat surprising capitulation, for the foolish young gentlemen had already spent considerably more than this pretty specimen of genteel poverty ever would. "Tom, take it back to the pen."

Obligingly, the tapster put down his tray of ale and swept the little goat up under his arm, marching out the door with it, much to the vocal disappointment of its tormentors.

"How can I help you, miss?" the innkeeper asked through these protestations.

The noise increased again and Illsworth lost the beginning of the conversation until the girl's voice rose too. "I bespoke a bedchamber *and* a private parlour!"

"Huzzah!" cried most of the young men across the room.

The girl spared none of them a glance. Her eyes remained rivetted to the innkeeper's face.

"You don't want to stay here, miss," he said, shocked. "Not tonight. You'd hate it!"

"I will hate it," she agreed. "However, I shall hate seeking shelter beneath a hedge even more."

"The other thing is, miss, there's no rooms free."

"But I wrote to you reserving the rooms a fortnight ago!"

"Before the fight was arranged," Wriggley said wisely. "Can't have known we'd all show up."

"Then my rooms were reserved first, and I insist on the bedchamber I was promised. I am prepared to forgo the private parlour."

"Come and be private with me," said one of the goat wagerers, sidling over to her lasciviously, much to the loud amusement of his friends, one of whom stepped to the girl's other side and slipped his arm around her waist.

Several men laughed and whistled. Illsworth couldn't see what happened next, but the youth suddenly dropped his arm with a strangled grunt. Someone shoved him aside and took his place. Others pressed closer.

"You see how it is, miss," the innkeeper said helplessly. "My hands are tied, and you and your family'd be a sight safer under that hedge. Look, there's a smaller house only two miles down the road. Mrs. Harbottle'll look after you there."

"We'll look after you better here," shouted Durward, always one to stir the pot for a pretty face.

"I am not walking two miles in the rain with all our baggage," the girl exclaimed. "I insist on having the room I was promised!"

"Huzzah!" cheered the crowd once more.

The goat wagerer flung an arm around her and kissed her cheek, then dodged back as if avoiding a boxing hit. The room roared with laughter. Illsworth allowed himself a tolerant smile.

Sanderly sighed and stood up.

"Sirs, let the lady be and go back to your ale," the harassed innkeeper said as Sanderly strolled across the room and the men began shoving each other out of the way to crowd closer to the girl. Somehow, though, a path cleared for Sanderly. The girl, who was now clutching her battered carpet bag very tightly indeed, finally saw him.

She glared repellingly, tilting her chin as though recognizing a more dangerous animal than those nearest her who, like a pack of curs, were egging each other on with lewd barks and nips.

"Give her a squeeze, Snake!" some wag encouraged to more raucous laughter.

Snake did more than that. He stood very close to her, and she could not retreat for the surrounding men. He placed one finger under her chin, almost as though he were about to inspect her teeth, then pounced, fastening his lips to hers. His free hand held her by the nape to keep her head steady.

The men began to stamp in appreciation, though those nearest were objecting vociferously that they were there first.

Snake raised his head in a leisurely fashion. "Why, yes, you shall share my room," he announced, then, as she seemed about to spit with fury, "No, darling, you shall thank me in the morning."

The girl's eyes widened. She closed her mouth, staring at him, but he was already walking away from her. A gurgling breath escaped her, which, astonishingly, sounded like laughter. Hardly a flattering response to Sanderly's kiss, or his highly improper invitation, but Sanderly's only reaction was the faintest twitch of the lips.

"Have Mrs. George see to it," he said to the innkeeper. "I'm playing dice."

Chapter Two

For once in her life, Miss Harriet Cole was deprived of words. Not because of the insolence of her handsome tormentor, nor his almost frighteningly intense blue eyes, nor even the shock of being kissed for the first time in her life in *such* a way.

What forced her smothered giggle and took her by complete surprise was the cold metal that he slid into her palm at the same time. He had given her the key to his room.

And if he imagined she would open the door to him or anyone else that night, he was vastly mistaken. Even more insultingly, as soon as he'd kissed her, he appeared to forget the whole matter and return his focus to the dice game.

Around her, men were castigating him for muscling in, addressing him in high dudgeon as "my lord," "Sanderly," or "Snake," depending on how loud their voices. He did not appear to notice, merely sat down and threw the dice with a practised, elegant flick of his wrist.

Someone grasped her by the arm. "This way, miss," said a large, grim-looking woman, presumably the innkeeper's wife, urging her toward the stairs. One man fell to his knees beseechingly. Another blew her a kiss. But noticeably, they kept their distance now, as if *his* mark was upon her. She was grateful for that too, since a press of people always upset her and she had been about to panic before he intervened.

His mark, *his* key. *Her* room.

"Wait, I need to fetch the children," she said, pulling back. "I can't let them pass through *that*—"

"Tom'll bring 'em up the back stairs and lock the door behind." Mrs. George hauled herself on to the landing and using her own set of keys, opened the first door on the left.

"Lucky bastard," said a voice feelingly at the foot of the stairs.

"Ignore 'em," Mrs. George said roughly. "Nice as ninepence when they ain't jug-bitten. Like a pack of animals right now, though, all wound up by a stupid prize fight and more ale inside 'em than my newly stocked cellars."

A lamp was already lit. Mrs. George turned it up and took a spill to light some candles. Harriet looked about her. A closed trunk sat under the window. A hairbrush seemed to have been thrown carelessly on the bed, on top of a discarded coat. A leather bag was open beside it.

"Who is that man?" Harriet asked, dropping her own tatty carpet bag on the floor.

"Earl of Sanderly."

"He doesn't look like a man who gets drunk at prize fights."

"He's certainly not sober. Didn't come for the fight, though, just went because he was here. Never thought he'd put up with that lot."

"Yet you didn't give *his* room away."

Mrs. George glanced at her with what might have been apology. "Didn't think you'd come once you heard about the fight, or want to stay if you did."

"I don't," Harriet said ruefully. "But my sister's not well and I don't want to make her walk two miles in the rain and the dark—certainly not with men like that springing out from every hedge."

"Oh, I think they're all safe under cover," Mrs. George said, tossing the hairbrush and the coat into the open bag on the bed. She looked around for any other items and removed a shaving kit from the washstand. "I'll send you up some tea and a hot meal—if they've left any. Tom'll take the trunk away."

Harriet, who'd had every intention of shoving both bag and trunk out into the passage herself, eyed Mrs. George with unease. "Won't he mind your removing his things?"

"Don't be daft, he meant me to, didn't he? Otherwise he wouldn't have sent me up with you."

Harriet closed her mouth. Had he given her the key not to let her in but to keep everyone else out? Then why the performance downstairs? Opportunism?

"Where will *he* sleep?" And why did she care now?

Mrs. George cast her a look. "You think any of us'll get any sleep? You'd have been better at the Red Lion. You might want to leave early in the morning while they're finally out cold."

"Oh, I mean to, and that reminds me, can you provide us with a conveyance to Grand Court?"

Mrs. George paused by the bedchamber door. "Grand Court?"

She sounded so disbelieving that Harriet tilted her chin. "Lady Grandison is my godmother."

"And she couldn't send someone to meet you off the *stagecoach*?" She uttered the last word with such contempt that Harriet would have blushed had she not been so tired.

"I do not care to trouble her," she said haughtily, before she became aware of heavy footsteps in the hall and grabbed her carpet bag again. At a pinch it would make a useful weapon, although Mrs. George herself might prove to be a better one.

The innkeeper's wife pulled open the door and Harriet's sisters and cousin spilled into the room ahead of the tapster carrying their bags.

"Oh, Harry, did you see the baby goat?" Rose said. "Its mother was crying for it, and you should have seen it dashing and jumping around to find her. So sweet!"

"Trunk, Tom," Mrs. George said.

"Lord, have we thrown someone out of their room?" Alex asked with more cheer than guilt.

"I thought so," Harriet murmured, casting her bonnet on the large bed, "but apparently not." Her first concern, when the door closed behind Mrs. George, Tom, and the trunk, was Lily, who looked very pale and wan. "Does your head still hurt?"

"Only a little," Lily assured her. "The fresh air helped, and that sweet little goat made me feel better."

"There's an awful racket downstairs," Orchid remarked, reaching for the door handle. She was only six years old. "I'll just nip down and see what's going—"

"Absolutely not," Harriet said, so forcefully that they all gawped at her. "There is a large party of—er...sporting gentlemen at the inn and they are...not at their best."

"Foxed?" Rose suggested.

Harriet gave in. "Drunk as wheelbarrows," she admitted. "And horrible to be around. You are not to leave this room for anything less than fire. I'm serious, Orchid. They already tried to assault me."

"Oh, did they?" Alex demanded, his face kindling with wrath.

Harriet, who should have remembered her cousin's newly protective instincts now that he was all of ten years old, hastily assured him that no harm was done and that the gentleman concerned had apologised. "In his own way," she added, fitting the key he had given her into the lock.

Alex seemed mollified, although when the sharp rap sounded on the door, he marched up to open it first, with Harriet at his heels. However, their visitor was merely Tom, with a large heavy tray which he placed on the table.

He bade them good night with a certain wistfulness before he squared his shoulders and returned to the chaos downstairs. Harriet locked the door behind him.

There were only two chairs at the table, so they all sat on the floor, while Harriet sliced the pie and divided up the vegetables that came with it.

"Eat as much as you can," she urged Lily, who was eyeing her plate without enthusiasm. "And then you can go to bed. Hopefully the rabble below will fall into a collective stupor soon and give us some peace."

"Over-optimistic," Rose pronounced. "Cousin Randolph's friends don't fall asleep until dawn sometimes. And if you ask me, it's not their discussions of the Bible or philosophy that makes them gabble so much."

Cousin Randolph, in fact, was the epitome of hypocrisy. He preached a rigid Puritan code of hard work, simple fare, and modest dress for his wards, but possessed a rather magnificent wardrobe for a clergyman. He also had some distinctly raffish acquaintances who didn't come often to the house, although he travelled frequently to London to see them. On church business, apparently, although he had no living of his own.

"I wonder if he's missed us yet?" Alex wondered.

"Bound to have," Rose said, "when his dining table won't have set itself or the candles sprung magically to life when he wants them. I wish I could see his face when he realizes his unpaid housekeeper and servants have gone…"

Rose was still at the "serves him right" stage. But Lily's eyes were sad as she met Harriet's gaze. Already, she was missing her old home. Harriet's own heart twisted at the thought of leaving it in Randolph's hands, but the law had made him the owner on their father's death. And in truth, they had no reason to stay.

"Do you suppose Lady Grandison will be happy to see us?" Orchid asked.

"Bound to be." Alex grinned. "Just look at us! And we're pretty useful—I suppose we can thank Randolph for that if for nothing else."

"I'm not thanking him," Orchid said. "He's a pig."

Alex snorted in his best pig impersonation. Orchid replied and they all soon joined in, even Lily, laughing till their throats hurt.

Although Lily hadn't eaten a great deal, she had drunk all her tea and she did not resist when everyone else urged her into bed. After that, they prepared for the night in order of age.

From below came shouts and gales of laughter and occasional inexplicable bumps and crashes, the tinkle of breaking glass and massive cheers. Sometimes a voice was raised in anger. Then the fiddle music began, along with a thunderous stomping that made everyone giggle helplessly with images of the drunken jigging below.

"Do you suppose all the gentlemen are dancing with each other?" Rose said.

"There are some women there," Harriet said, recalling with distaste her glimpse of the woman on some man's knee being fondled quite inappropriately while the same man gaped lasciviously at Harriet. The woman had glared at her too.

"Are they foxed?" Orchid asked with interest.

"Ladies don't get foxed," Alex said disparagingly from the truckle bed no doubt designed for servants.

Harriet decided to say nothing. She climbed into bed beside her sisters, blew out the last candle and lay down.

It was going to be a long night. Still, she had plenty to think about, planning just the right words to explain to Lady Grandison why they had come to her and how to enlist her help in the matter of schools and a governess position, and secrecy. Then there was the embarrassing necessity of borrowing money for travel, for they'd used their last penny in getting this far. Even the cost of the hired chaise tomorrow would have to be borne by Sir John Grandison. And then there was how to appease her employer for the sad fact of her youth.

All these things required planning, and yet her wayward mind kept being distracted by a dark, haughty, devastatingly handsome face with the most stunning eyes she had ever seen. The touch of his fingers on her skin, and the shock of his mouth on hers. She was outraged at such disrespect, furious at the assault by a so-called gentleman, a nobleman. *With nothing noble about him*, she told herself crossly.

And yet he had given her his key and apparently issued some kind of silent order for his things to be removed.

If he had wanted her to have his room, why had he not simply offered as a gentleman should? Why the show? And it *had* been a show, she realized, not without an inexplicable feeling of insult. Was it possible he had been deliberately hiding a good deed in a bad one? Why would he do that?

She supposed she would never know. But she *could* be grateful to him, and she was...

THE EARL OF SANDERLY knew he was in danger of being lulled into a false sense of security. Once the fiddler started, the noisy, drunken conviviality of the inn began to take on a familiar, comfortable aspect, almost like impromptu parties in the officers' mess at winter quarters in Portugal.

It must have been Jonny Berry's presence, making him maudlin for old times. In retrospect, they certainly weren't good times.

"Shall we increase the bet?" Illsworth said.

Sanderly shrugged. "If we all agree."

Beside him, Berry said, "I'm out, whatever you agree. Happy to watch for a bit, though. Never could see the skill in this game."

"There isn't any," Durward said cheerfully. "That's what makes it exciting. Pure luck, to make you rich or ruin you."

"It's certainly ruining me," Wolf said.

"Stop playing then," Sanderly advised. "I'll take the bank."

No doubt the flicker of alarm in Illsworth's eyes was reflected in the others, which made Sanderly smile with as much of a sneer as he could fit into a gentle curl of the lips.

"If no one objects," he purred.

It was ridiculous. No one played with a cheat. One cut him dead until he was too humiliated to be seen in public. Yet here Sanderly was, not only playing but winning at hazard against a table full of drunks, and no one had accused him of loading the dice.

Yet. The night was young.

Illsworth chose to be gracious, though a few minutes later, he said, "I'm surprised to see you still here, with such a treat awaiting you in your bedchamber."

"Oh, I don't mind making her wait. Play."

They played.

Illsworth said, "Shall we see you at Lady Grandison's?"

"God, no," Sanderly said with a shudder.

"Lady Barbara will be there."

"I'm aware."

"Whatever persuaded you to give your beautiful sister to such a dull stick as Martindale?" Durward asked.

"She did. I really didn't care enough to argue. If we're going to gossip, I'm going to bed." He raised his eyes to see Wriggley edging up the stairs toward the bedchamber. "Going somewhere, Wriggles?"

A spasm crossed the man's face, although he froze with one foot on the next step. "Just going to the pot, old fellow," he said feebly.

"Go outside like everyone else," Sanderly recommended.

"There's no need to be such a damned dog in the manger," Wriggley said.

"You've got no right to guard her like a bone, Snake," someone else called. "Sharing is an act of friendship."

"I agree," Sanderly said sweetly. "No one touches her."

"Or what, my lord?" Illsworth asked in clear amusement.

Sanderly merely curled his lip. He'd made his point. Jonny, however, backed it up by laying a pistol heavily on the table. *Talk about a damned sledgehammer…*

A few shocked laughs rippled around the room among those still paying attention. Wriggley was back at the foot of the stairs.

"Bit excessive, old man," Illsworth said to Jonny.

"Who the devil is he?" Wriggley blustered. "Your guard dog?"

"What is this fixation on dogs?" Sanderly wondered. "And of course he is not. In fact, he's the best shot of the 95th—never misses. He lost half a leg at Salamanca. Didn't stop him reloading and shooting the enemy into submission. Are you going to throw those dice, Wolf, or just keep praying to them?"

There were no more efforts to go upstairs, except when the weaker-headed gentlemen began to fall over and were carried to bed by their friends and the tapster. Others had a blanket thrown over them in what had once been a private parlour.

"You headed for Harwich, Snake?" Durward asked, stuffing his meagre winnings into his pocket. "I'll come with you."

"What, has Foster died?" Illsworth asked with interest.

"Not yet," Durward said gloomily. "Planning in advance."

"What has Foster's death to do with you?" asked Wolf, who must have been the only man present not to know about the duel.

"I shot him, didn't I?" Durward said bitterly. "They'll be after me for murder if he croaks."

"Afraid of the law, Durward?" Illsworth mocked.

"No, of my grandmother," Durward retorted. "And who wouldn't be?"

"Fair point," Sanderly allowed.

"Well, we'll think of you in Harwich at some run-down wharfside inn," Wolf said, standing up, "while we are enjoying the legendary hospitality of Lady Grandison."

"One more round, gentlemen?" Sanderly suggested.

Fortunately, everyone else finally seemed to be as bored as he was. The riotous inn had descended into snores and snuffles and the distant sound of retching.

Goerge the innkeeper was dousing the rest of the lights. Through the windows came the first glimmering of dawn.

Thank God. Sanderly stretched his legs, one at a time, and rose to his feet.

Mrs. George stood at the foot of the stairs. She must have taken a liking to the girl to be guarding her.

"I'll pay my shot now," he said.

"I won't include the room."

Sanderly sighed. "Include the room."

Mrs. George's eyes gleamed. "She wants a chaise to Grand Court tomorrow. I don't think she's a clue what it will cost her."

He paused. "Then I hope Lady Grandison is pleased to see her."

"That's what I said. And with all those children too. Apparently her ladyship is her godmother."

"Is she, by God?" Sanderly murmured, following Mrs. George to the front of the house, where she scribbled what looked like a random amount on a docket beside his name. He placed a handful of coins on top of it with equal randomness. "Thank you."

"Going there yourself, my lord?" Mrs. George inquired. "Lots of these gents seem to be."

"Harwich gets more appealing by the instant. Are my bags back in my carriage?"

"They are, my lord."

He was half out of the door before another random thought struck him. "How many children are there?"

"Four. Five counting her."

She was no child, though almost certainly sheltered and gently born. Pity, in many ways, but there it was.

He walked out of the inn into the cold, grey morning. He wondered if the girl found siblings the same curse he did.

His stomach twisted with the same old pain. He wouldn't allow it to be his heart. But Christ, he missed Hugo.

I'm drunk. I'm tired. And it's time for pastures new. I'm off to Africa...

At the stables, he sent a yawning lad in search of his coachman and went to fetch his own horses for speed.

A figure loomed up from the straw, startling him. The lantern light played over the features of a young and entirely unexpected man. *None of my business.*

"Morning, your Grace," he murmured.

"Good morning, my lord."

Ignoring each other, they fetched their own horses.

Sanderly tried to talk himself out of the idea. He should never have thought of Hugo, because it reminded him of Bab, his one remaining sibling. And his mild curiosity about the girl who was apparently Eliza Grandison's goddaughter, was entirely irrelevant. Jennings, his coachman, and the sleepy stable lad finished harnessing the horses to the carriage. But as Jennings held the carriage door for him, he finally sighed and gave in.

"Grand Court first, I'm afraid, Jennings. I believe I must call upon my sister. Can you imagine Lady Grandison's delight?"

"Vividly, my lord," Jennings said, perfectly wooden.

Sanderly bestowed a nod of approval upon him and climbed into the carriage.

Chapter Three

Lord Illsworth, who had drunk less than most, rose earlier than all but the sorry gentlemen who had collapsed first in one of the private parlours, and were now holding their heads in the aired common room and making heavy weather of their hearty breakfasts.

Give Sanderly his due, he would definitely have known how to extract the most humour from this moment. Illsworth, spying the immoderate young gentlemen over the balustrade from the landing above, merely allowed himself a smug smile. *There but for the grace of God...*

He straightened and went on toward the stairs. He had come out slightly ahead last night, though hardly enough to sustain him through the deep gaming at Lady Grandison's. He would have to be creative.

At the head of the stairs, he paused, for the door to Sanderly's room was open. On impulse, he strolled along to it and knocked, gently pushing. The door opened wider to reveal that the room was entirely empty. Both girl and earl had gone. Unless they were braving the lewd sniggers in the coffee room. He doubted the sorry specimens he'd glimpsed were up to much ribald teasing, but Illsworth could manage a few pithy shots.

He was about to leave again when he noticed the paper propped up on the mantel shelf. Curious, he walked into the room and picked it up. It was directed to Lord Sanderly and unsealed. Which was basically an invitation to look.

He unfolded the missive, which was brief and written in a hurried if well-formed hand.

My lord,

Please accept my thanks for your generosity last night.

Followed by some illegible squiggle of a signature that he could not read.

What the devil did it mean? Illsworth wondered in some distaste. That the man was a generous lover and paid well? And the lout hadn't even taken her letter with him!

Mind you, he had probably left as soon as he'd finished with her. He had been bending the elbow rather more than usual...

"Who cares?" he muttered, stuffing the note in his pocket. He had a habit of collecting things that might prove useful later. Even if Snake was leaving the country, it could be something to hold over his delectable sister. Should she prove recalcitrant, though he had no reason to suppose she would.

His blood warmed pleasantly at the thought of her, and he went down to breakfast in a much better mood. Tonight, he thought, would be his night.

SINCE HE DID NOT PLAN to stay more than an hour or so at Grand Court, Sanderly stopped at the local village inn to break his fast. It was a quiet place, unused to gentlemen travellers who tended to stay at the bigger posting inns or with the Grandisons, who were known to be hospitable people.

The flustered innkeeper's wife seated him at her best table and fussed over him. The maid who served him gawped so hard she spilled his tea. He bore it all with patience, since the food was excellent and even the giggling was likely to be less annoying than whatever it was his sister had to say to him. He even contemplated changing his mind and going on instead to Harwich, but he had already come this far and perhaps he really should look in on her if he was going to be away for several years.

So, he climbed back into his carriage and was driven the short distance to Grand Court. Of course, it was not yet nine of the clock, far too early to expect his hosts to receive him, which suited Sanderly well enough.

He presented his card to a very superior butler. "Lady Barbara Martindale, if you please."

The butler bowed. Titles did not overwhelm him. "I'll inquire if her ladyship is abroad."

"She won't be," Sanderly said dryly. "Have her maid wake her and tell her I shall only be here for the next hour."

"Very good, my lord." The butler departed into the depths of the house, leaving Sanderly to kick his heels in the entrance hall. He passed the time examining the paintings of Grandison's Friday faced ancestors, and decided they were almost as gruesome as his own.

However, he did not have long to wait before a woman he vaguely recognized hurried across the hall and curtseyed to him. "My lord. Her ladyship asks if you will step upstairs to her chamber."

Sanderly sighed. "Lead on." It was either that or wait two hours for her to dress.

As soon as the maid opened the bedroom door, Barbara flew up in a haze of lace, grasping his arm in a vice-like grip, and dragged him into the room.

"Go away, Masters," she flung at the maid.

"I'll go with her if you're going to abuse my poor coat," Sanderly warned.

She all but flung his arm from her. "Oh, Snake, a plague on your wretched coat!"

"And on whatever problem inspired your summons," he said affably, looking her up and down. She was dressed in some kind of frothy dressing gown over an even frothier night gown. "You look like a cake."

Her giggle was unexpected and surprisingly welcome, although she quickly frowned at him again. "Have you come just to insult me?"

"No, I came because you said I should, and I had a free hour to kill. What do you want, Bab?"

"Oh, Snake, you just *have* to talk to James and—"

"Who is James?" he interrupted, wandering over to the window and sniffing at the vase of fresh flowers there.

She stared at him with dislike. "My husband!"

"Ah. *Dear* James."

"You needn't say it like that!"

"Like what? You assured me he would become dear to me. I am doing my best."

"You are being sarcastic and nasty. You were never like that before Hugo died."

He made his smile as wintry and unpleasant as he could. "I am living up to expectations. But I am a man of simple ideas. For instance, *you* talk to dearest James, who is, as you pointed out, *your* husband."

For a moment, she seemed likely to fly off the handle. Extracting a dainty, pink rose from the vase, he held it under his nose, watching with some interest as she struggled to master her temper and, surprisingly, won. Clearly, she was serious.

"You do delight in provoking people, don't you, Snake? Well, I shan't hold it against you if you will just hear me out. I want you to talk to James *and* Illsworth."

"Illsworth? I've said more than enough to him today already."

"Oh God, is he coming here?"

Sanderly pretended to think about it while he watched her face. "Is he? Yes, I believe he said so."

"Oh, the devil, then you absolutely have to speak to both of them."

"Do I? And what exactly is it I'm supposed to say to both of them?"

She spun around and threw herself onto the chaise longue. "I want you to tell James that my affections are fixed and loyal and that I did not marry him merely to gain the freedoms of a married woman. And I want you tell Illsworth to give me back the cravat pin I gave him. And destroy any letters I may have written to him."

Sanderly stared at her. "If you wanted the inestimable Illsworth, why the devil did you nag me so mercilessly to let you marry dear James?"

"Illsworth must marry money," she said miserably.

"How very vulgar, but since you began it, allow me to point out that you were never a pauper."

"Well, he needs a positively *vulgar* amount—a cit's daughter, in fact—but that's not the point. I didn't want to marry Cedric."

"Cedric," Sanderly repeated. "Now I am entirely confused. Who is Cedric?"

She spared him a withering glance, although a hint of colour rose to her pale cheeks. "Cedric is Illsworth's Christian name, as you very well know. I have been acquainted with him forever and never had the remotest desire to marry him. It was always James."

"Dear James," Sanderly murmured, but if Bab noticed, she did not rise to the bait.

"The thing is, Snake," she said carefully. "I have done something very foolish."

"No!" he uttered in polite disbelief. It won him no more than the briefest glance of irritation. She really was serious enough to inspire his first twinge of genuine unease. "What did you do?"

"I gave Cedric Illsworth a present."

"What sort of present? A valuable one, I assume."

"It is to me," she whispered, then cleared her throat. "It was the first token of love James gave to me—pray, don't pretend you will be sick!"

"I wasn't going to. I am much too flabbergasted by your...I don't even know what to call it. Bad taste? Bad form? Idiocy?"

"Idiocy will do," she said miserably. "I was just so angry with James. I love him madly, of course, but he can be so wretchedly staid and - and judgmental and..."

"And you lost your temper and gave his token to Illsworth just to annoy him."

"I did," she agreed, apparently relieved by his understanding. "The thing is, I tried to do so in front of James—we were at the Larchester ball at the time, but it turns out…" She met Sanderly's gaze now with some indignation. "He didn't even notice!"

"How very disobliging of him. I do hope everyone else at the ball observed your generosity."

"Oh, stop it," she said with an impatient flick of her hand. "It was done lightly and discreetly and only James was supposed to notice by watching *me*."

"I warned you he would disappoint you."

"Don't be horrid, Snake. In any case, as soon as I had done it, I regretted it, for I *do* value the pin. I often wear at as a brooch for it is rather pretty, and more than that, it was the cravat pin James wore the first night I met him."

"Now, I might be sick. I suppose you asked Illsworth for it back and he'd already pawned it or lost it at hazard."

"No, he wrote back that he treasures it too much to return it and will wear it as a token of his love the next time we meet."

"When even James will notice."

"Precisely."

"I suppose you know you have lamentable taste in men."

"I must since you are my last hope."

"You want me to get the pin back from Illsworth."

"If you please," Bab said anxiously. "And, if you could, convince James that I have always been a faithful wife, and always will be."

"Are you?" Sanderly drawled.

Her eyes spat. "Of course I am! I only flirted with Illsworth to make James jealous, and he knew that…until he saw the letter."

Sanderly sat in the window seat and cast his eyes to heaven, gently wafting himself with the rose. "The letter," he repeated. "Illsworth's letter declaring his undying love for you?"

She nodded miserably. "He didn't mean it, of course. Cedric just likes to be in fashion while he pursues his heiress who is very unlikely to be remotely fashionable. But unfortunately, he is given to hyperbole and referred to our dance the previous evening as our night-time embrace and James..."

Sanderly raised his quizzing glass and regarded her through it. "I used to have a healthy regard for your intelligence, Bab. Marriage seems to have turned you perfectly bird-witted."

"I know," she said huskily. "I have made a huge mess of things, made my husband distrust me and given false evidence of misbehaviour to a man I wish I *hadn't* trusted."

"I wish you hadn't either," Sanderly said. "He most assuredly is not trustworthy as I'm sure dear James knows very well. However, I seem to recall you twist your husband around your little finger—one of the reasons I was against the match—so I'm surprised you have not done so."

"Well, I have, *up to a point*," Bab said. "But things are a little...*fragile* between us. If he finds out I gave Illsworth the brooch, if he sees him wearing it in front of everyone here at Grand Court... Some of them will recognize it as mine."

"I see."

"I knew you would. It will humiliate James, wreck my marriage, and spoil my good name. And yours, by association."

He refocused on her. "Don't be ridiculous. My name was spoiled long since. In fact, the only reason I consented to dear James in the end was the fact that he was prepared to take you in the teeth of my reputation."

"You see?" she said proudly. "He isn't as staid as you think him."

"He doesn't need to be staid to object to this particular mess."

"No, I know, and normally I wouldn't involve you, but the thing is, I don't want to be alone with Illsworth in order to plead with him in person."

"The first sensible thing you have said this morning."

She swallowed. Humility did not come easily to any of his family. "I know. So will you help me, Snake?"

"I only have an hour," he said, as the bleakness threatened to fold around him again. "I have a ship that will not wait for me."

She sat up, a sharp frown tugging her perfectly arched eyebrows. "What, you're not *really* fleeing the country, are you?"

"I'm going to Africa."

"*Africa?* But why? You're a peer of the realm. The law can barely touch you for anything. Did you kill someone in a duel? Never tell me you're *really* afraid of a few husbands shooting you!"

Sanderly regarded his almost perfectly manicured fingernails with mild disfavour. "I thank you for the loyalty, of course, but I don't much care whether cowardice—"

"You were never a coward, Snake," she interrupted with unexpected ferocity.

It spoke volumes for his need of escape that this limited accolade from his little sister actually brought a lump to his throat. He stood up and strolled toward her, presenting her with the rose.

"But I am, my dear. I'm mortally afraid of crashing boredom if nothing else."

For an instant, he was horribly afraid he saw understanding in her eyes, but it might have just been hopelessness.

She snatched the rose from his fingers. "Can't you take a later ship? Next week, next month? You're the only one I can trust, Snake."

He stared back at her. "Silly question, Bab—why don't you trust your husband?"

Her breath shuddered. "Because he doesn't trust me."

What a mess. What a bloody silly mess.

"Can't we think our way out of it?" she wheedled. "You were always the best at thinking."

No, I wasn't. Hugo was.

He paced toward the door, mainly to outrun the thought.

"Oh God," Bab said behind him, springing to her feet and rushing to the window. "I hear a carriage arriving. I'll bet that's Illsworth."

"Nonsense. It's nowhere near midday."

"Besides, it's a post-chaise and he generally drives himself. Oh look, Snake, it's a parcel of ragged children! What on earth are they doing at Grand Court? Do you suppose they're Sir John's long-lost love-children pursuing their birthrights?"

"Have you ever thought of novel writing?" he asked disparagingly.

But for no reason, his spirits lifted. He strolled back across the room in time to see the girl in the familiar if execrable straw hat square her shoulders and lead the gaggle of children toward the front door. They reminded him of a line of ducklings following their mother. Which might have been why he wanted to smile.

Instead, he sighed. "I suppose I still have another hour."

Chapter Four

The post chaise deposited the Cole family at the front door of Grand Court in the late morning. It was an impressively large, gracious house with a Grecian portico and dizzying rows of windows, mostly with closed curtains.

"Fine ladies rise late," Lily noted.

"But it's nearly eleven," Alex objected, pushing open the carriage door and dropping the step. "Someone should be up."

Someone was. A liveried footman made his stately way down the front steps, instructing the postilion where to take the carriage in order to be paid and find refreshment. Which was the first weight off Harriet's mind.

"Thank you," she said to the footman, trying not to sound too relieved. "Please inform Lady Grandison that Miss Cole is here. I'm afraid I foolishly forgot my cards."

This lie was lost in the footman's appalled stare as he took in their meagre, tattered baggage, the number of children and mended patches on their clothes, and finally, Harriet's poor hat and the old fashioned, mended gown beneath the thin travelling cloak that was too short for her.

Harriet tilted her chin. "Now, if you please. We shall wait indoors."

The haughty footman might have objected had she not already started walking briskly up the steps to the front door, the children at her heels. Of course, the servant would not shout.

"Her ladyship is not yet abroad," the footman declared breathlessly as he entered the hall with their bags. Obviously, he thought what he had to say justified the solecism of bringing baggage in by the front entrance. "What's more, she's entertaining a large party of friends."

"From her bed?" Orchid asked with genuine interest.

Alex and Rose snorted with laughter.

At which point a much more severe figure appeared, bowing expressionlessly.

"Miss Cole," the footman blurted to this august personage with a bizarre mixture of misery and outrage that made Harriet want to giggle. "Asking for her ladyship."

"Miss Cole," the butler repeated thoughtfully.

Harriet met his gaze. "Miss Harriet Cole. These are my sisters and my cousin."

"Of course. Welcome to Grand Court. Perhaps you would care to await her ladyship in the small salon."

Having pointed the footman to the back of the hall with the luggage, the butler led Harriet and the children to a small but ornate room on the left of the front door. Harriet suspected this was where problem callers were put, those whom the Grandisons might not turn away but whom they wished not to intrude on other guests. At the same time, the butler *had* seemed to recognize her name…

"It's a pity we're not used to visiting here," Lily observed. There was a worrying, slightly hectic flush to her cheeks that Harriet didn't like. Lily needed to be in bed and dosed with feverfew. "Lady Grandison always came to us."

"Always used to," Harriet murmured. Her ladyship had last descended upon them more than three years ago, in the wake of their mother's sudden death. She had written, of course…

A flurry of quick footsteps approached in company with an expensive rustling of silk, and Lady Grandison swept into the room in a positive haze of perfume and gauze. She still favoured a vast array of the lightest, most exquisite shawls that enfolded her like a cloud as she advanced upon Harriet.

"My dear, what an unexpected pleasure!" she exclaimed, embracing Harriet. "I could not believe it when Mitchell told me you were here. All of you! Lily, my pet, you are growing so beautiful! Rose, so tall! Orchid? Goodness, I would never have known you! And Alex, too, quite the young gentleman."

They were all embraced in turn. Even Orchid, who understood the importance of the event, refrained from grimacing or wriggling.

"Sit down while you tell me all!" Lady Grandison said, beaming, and flapping her hands towards the various chairs, which looked too spindly to be sat on. "Did you write to me Harriet? For if you did, I have been most horribly remiss and forgotten! You see, I am in the midst of this party, and there has been so much correspondence and such activity..."

"Oh dear," Harriet said uneasily. "Your footman did say you had guests, but I thought he was just trying to be rid of us more easily. I suppose we are quite a bag full of rags."

Lady Grandison seemed to take in their appearance for the first time as she sat down and looked around them all with growing unease.

"Well, no one wears their best to travel any distance," she excused them, then brightened again. "I don't know why I didn't think of simply inviting you to the party! I had quite forgotten you were grown up, Harriet—you must be more than, what, seventeen?"

"I am nineteen, ma'am."

A guilty, almost hunted look entered her ladyship's expression. "Oh dear. And I promised your dear mama I would sponsor your come-out. Well, it is never too late for a Season, though it will have to be next year now..."

"Oh, no, my lady," Harriet said hastily. "A Season is quite out of the question."

"Nonsense. I shall write to your guardian and explain that neither the bother nor the expense will touch him, and you shall come and live in London with me..."

"My lady, I cannot leave the children."

She blinked, eyeing them doubtfully, then said heroically, "Then they must come too. With their governess, of course..."

"We don't have a governess," Harriet said with difficulty. "The thing is, the whole of Gorsefield Park is entailed and it all belongs to Cousin Randolph."

"Yes, I know. It was a great concern to both your parents, which is why your good papa left you all a decent amount of money in funds and so on—"

"Which we cannot touch until we are five-and twenty," Harriet pointed out. "That is six more years in which we have nothing at all between us."

"No," Lady Grandison said, still bewildered, "but Randolph has given you a continued home with him, has he not?"

"That's the problem," Rose burst out. "He is *awful*."

Lady Grandison looked startled.

"He is," Harriet agreed. "No letters ever come to us anymore, and I have become convinced he never sends the ones we write. For example, how many letters have you received from me in the last year?"

Lady Grandison frowned. "Just the one informing me of your father's death, and I could not come to you for Amelia was lying in and then..."

"I wrote at least eight," Harriet said.

"Eight! I must have sent three or so, but when you did not reply..."

"You see?" Rose said triumphantly. "He is *evil*."

"Oh, my dear, that is a little harsh! One must not..."

"He is certainly unpleasant," Harriet said. "And...and *joyless*, and he is using us increasingly as servants. It has made Lily ill and that is unforgivable. To be frank, we have been little more than prisoners. Believe me, our escape to you had to be well-planned. What we came to ask of your ladyship is, first of all, secrecy."

"Secrecy?" she repeated.

"Hide us from Randolph," Harriet said bluntly. "Just for a few weeks. I have applied for a position as governess to a respectable family in Berkshire and I'm afraid I gave them your address. I—er... also rely on your ladyship for a character."

Lady Grandison closed her gaping mouth, swallowed, and said faintly, "But what of the younger ones, my dear?"

"I shall pay for them to go to school," Harriet said.

"From your salary," Lady Grandison said slowly, "as a governess."

Harriet smiled upon her. "It is a clever plan, is it not? I don't quite like that Alex would be on his own while he is still so young, but the girls would all be able to look after each other, and if you wouldn't *very* much mind having them for holidays sometimes when I cannot get leave of absence...?"

She broke off as two footmen entered with trays full of lemonade and tea, bread and butter, scones and biscuits. The children's eyes lit up. Harriet rather thought her godmother was relieved not to have to think for a few minutes. She was the best natured of creatures, which was why Harriet had dared to impose upon her, but she had the distinct feeling now that Lady Grandison did not approve of her plan at all.

"We cannot go back to Cousin Randolph," she said firmly, as soon as the door was closed behind the servants, just to nip that possibility in the bud.

"No, no, dear, I quite see that," her ladyship murmured. "I was never so shocked in my life. I must say I am surprised at your papa—always such a sensible man—for naming such a creature as your guardian."

"I suppose it made sense to him since Randolph would inherit Gorsefield Park anyway."

"He is a relatively young man, is he not? I suppose he cannot have liked to be saddled with so many children..."

"Then why did he not send them to school?" Harriet said. "As it is, their education, such as it is, has been up to me."

Lady Grandison nodded slowly. She appeared to be deep in thought, a process that did not come naturally to her. Finally, as Alex reached for a third scone, she nodded with decision.

"I shall consult with Sir John on the best way forward. For now, of course you must all stay as my honoured guests."

"What if Randolph comes here?" Orchid asked uneasily.

Lady Grandison smiled. "My dear! Sir John and I are quite capable of dealing with Randolph. Now, the question is, how to deal with you?" She looked them all over once more. "You really *are* a bag full of rags, aren't you? We must change that as quickly as possible, especially for you, Harriet, if you are to join in the party."

"I would much rather be useful to you, ma'am."

"But you will be. Mitchell tells me I have another unexpected guest, so without you, my numbers are all upset. Now, what ails poor Lily?"

In no time, Lily was ensconced in one of the comfortable beds in what was to be Harriet's room, a pretty apartment that had lately belonged to Lady Grandison's daughter Amelia. Propped up on pillows and sipping willow bark tea, Lily watched as wide-eyed as the others as two maids paraded past her ladyship with a vast array of gowns, hats, shawls, pelisses, reticules, boots, outdoor shoes, and slippers.

In household matters, Lady Grandison could clearly focus on several things at once, which might have been difficult for others to follow, but did not appear to trouble her ladyship.

"The emerald green for certain, Nesbit. I'm afraid I must put you younger ones in the nursery, since there is so little room elsewhere, though I think you are quite right, Harriet, that Lily should stay with you until she is quite well again. Ah, the white silk we can do something with. I had better assign Mildred to the nursery and winkle poor Nurse out of retirement. You must be kind to Nurse, children, though she will sleep most of the day, but mind Mildred, for she is... Definitely the printed muslin, Nesbit, delightful for sunny afternoons and such suitable colours for you, Harriet dear. It never suited Amelia above half...

Easy going but eminently sensible. Alex can have the small room on the left, and the two girls could share the bigger room on the right. The dark blue riding habit, definitely. Bring pins, Millie. We shall go up directly..."

Orchid giggled, which set off the others, including Harriet and Lady Grandison. Even the maids had begun to smile when the bedchamber door opened and Sir John Grandison looked in.

"Eliza?" he said, clearly startled to find the room so full of people and activity. "What...?"

"Oh, come in Sir John, quickly. It is most exciting. Hetty Cole's daughters have come to stay. You do remember Harriet, my goddaughter? Poor Lily is unwell, and here are Rose and Orchid, whom you must have met before, and Alexander, who is their cousin. Freddie Cole took him in when his sister died, if you recall."

"Perfectly," Sir John said, beaming amiably. "Very happy you could come, though Eliza forgot to tell me."

"No, I didn't dear, but it has worked out for the best for our numbers were wrong now that Sanderly has turned up after all, and Harriet will make things right again—"

"Sanderly?" Harriet blurted before her godmother had finished her sentence. "The Earl of Sanderly is here?"

Lady Grandison looked uneasy. "Well, so Mitchell tells me, and he is never wrong. I believe he came to see Lady Barbara, who is his sister, so she must have persuaded him to stay. You needn't believe everything you hear about him, however. It is largely gossip."

"Which would have died down already if he didn't go out of his way to be unpleasant," Sir John said with more incomprehension than disapproval.

"He is always perfectly polite to me," Lady Grandison argued.

"Oh, and to everyone, but always with an *edge*."

"To be sure, he is given to sarcasm, which is not the pleasantest form of humour, but he can be terribly funny. John, you had best go away for Harriet must have at least one morning gown ready for luncheon."

"Of course she must," Sir John said, raising his hand to the children. "Welcome all! I'm just going down to breakfast."

"After eleven?" Orchid said in astonishment. "It's almost time for luncheon!"

"Which is why we must have Harriet's first gown fitted and resewn *tout de suite*!"

For Harriet, stupidly, the amusing idea of dressing up in Amelia's old clothes had suddenly taken on a new importance.

She wanted to thank the earl in person for the use of his room last night, but in a way that did not allude to his shocking behaviour. On no account must he even suspect that she remembered that insolent kiss, although she did, vividly, and with a confusing array of emotions that made her want to either slap him or hide. She was certain he would not have so insulted her had he known she was Lady Grandison's gently born goddaughter. And she hoped, by more stylish dress, to show him his mistake and inspire at least an apology if not a genuine regret.

Only she didn't like that either. A man who would so treat a friendless girl of no account in the world but apologise to a lady with important friends was really rather despicable. It was all rather confusing, and she didn't want to think about it anymore. In any case, she would be regal, gracious, and polite and then he would be sorry...

As Nesbit, Lady Grandison's personal maid, began to experiment with her hair, another thought struck her. She had not told anyone about her previous meeting with Lord Sanderly, for obvious reasons, but if he betrayed that he knew her, her silence would seem very odd.

I think too much. I shall merely be cool and polite and he will follow my lead. I may thank him in a mere moment when I get the chance, and that will be that.

The re-sewn dress was thrown over her freshly coiffured head, and Rose said in amazement, "Goodness, Harry, you look beautiful!"

Harriet laughed. Personal appearance had never mattered greatly to her—which was fortunate—but the new gown certainly improved her, and the complex hair arrangement fitted with the regal air she wished to convey.

Orchid, however, was scowling. "You don't look like you anymore."

"Then you are all far too used to quite unsuitable rags," Lady Grandison said roundly. "Honestly, I am surprised Randolph Cole was not ashamed to let you be seen!"

"We rarely were," Rose murmured. "Come on, Orchid, let's go and find Alex and the nursery."

"Mildred will bring you luncheon," Lady Grandison called after them, "and show you where you may play. Now, my dear, you will do splendidly, will she not, Lily?"

But Lily had fallen asleep and did not reply.

Harriet went to the bed and touched her sister's blessedly cool forehead before drawing the coverlet higher over her arms.

"She worries me," she confessed.

"Sleep is the best thing for her," Lady Grandison said comfortably. "She will be right as rain by tomorrow. And if she isn't, we shall summon Dr. Bagshott." She linked arms with Harriet, drawing her out of the room and along the passage to the stairs. "We have a delightfully full house, already, with just a couple more gentlemen due today. Luncheon is an informal meal and not everyone will attend, so it is a good time to begin to meet your fellow guests. Afterward, if the weather is still fine, we might play pall-mall on the lawn."

"Oh, the children will love that!"

Lady Grandison cast her a look. "Not for the children—at least not today. Perhaps tomorrow morning, or during excursions… I know you find it odd, but in Polite Society, people don't care to be bothered with children. Of course, they may play elsewhere in the garden at any time…"

"My lady, I am not criticizing," Harriet said hastily. "How could I? You have already been kindness itself when we have inflicted ourselves upon you most inconveniently in the midst of your party! I am just not used to such affairs and will probably say the wrong thing and embarrass you horribly."

"Nonsense, you have always been a charming, unaffected girl, and my guests will adore you. Luncheon is served in the garden room, just an informal buffet for a few people."

When they went downstairs together, the buzz and babble emanating from the garden room warned Harriet that her definition of "a few" was unlikely to be the same as her godmother's. And indeed, when the footman opened the door, a sea of people swam before her eyes.

Just for a second, the old memory flooded her with panic and she imagined them closing in on her, depriving her of safety and even breath...

Chapter Five

But of course, that could not happen here at Grand Court! Instead, while rising excitement, born of too much isolation, warred with fresh social anxiety, she reminded herself she was entitled to be here and no longer wore her embarrassing old gown.

Lady Grandison's clear pride in her helped. Holding on to Harriet's arm, her ladyship beamed around the room and spoke to the people immediately in front of them, two gentlemen and the most beautiful dark-haired lady Harriet had ever seen.

"Ah, you shall be the first to meet my favourite goddaughter, who has just joined us!" Lady Grandison said to the trio. "Allow me to present Miss Harriet Cole, the daughter of my dearest friend. Harriet, this is Mrs. Eldridge, Sir Ralph Lawrence who is our new member of parliament, and Mr. Thornton."

Harriet curtseyed to all and smiled at each introduction. The lovely Mrs. Eldridge regarded her without warmth and accorded her a slight inclination of the head, not so much unfriendly as indifferent. Sir Ralph, a handsome, fair gentleman, perhaps in his thirties, with a smiling face and rather sad eyes, bowed to her, as did the older Mr. Thornton, whose whole countenance gleamed with interest.

"Delighted, quite delighted," he said. "I look forward to our greater acquaintance."

"As do I," Sir Ralph Lawrence murmured.

He and Mr. Thornton stood aside to let them pass, and Harriet's stomach jolted hard.

Directly in front of her stood the tall, slender, supremely elegant figure of Lord Sanderly. His raven black hair swept down over his haughty brow in just the way she remembered. If his expression did not quite betray boredom, his posture did. The heavy eyelids rose, revealing the shock of those intensely blue eyes. He had no business having such eyes with that dark hair.

For a breathless moment, she was sure he looked right at her, and in spite of herself, she was pleased to see him and smiled. After all, she had vowed to express her gratitude as soon as she could, though she hadn't expected him to notice her quite so soon...

He hadn't.

As Lady Grandison drew her forward, his eyes remained fixed, not on Harriet after all, but on the lovely Mrs. Eldridge. Harriet felt her cheeks burn and tried to hold her smile in place.

Lord Sanderly's thin lips curved. He even inclined his head to Mrs. Eldridge. And then he turned to Lady Grandison, bowing.

"A thousand apologies, my lady," he said in the soft voice one could somehow never ignore. "Unforgivable to appear when I had already sent my regrets to your charming party."

"Nonsense, my lord!" Lady Grandison gave him her hand, which he bowed over punctiliously. "We are quite delighted to have you, as I hope Sir John intimated."

"Oh, he did, most hospitably." The words were civil, grateful, and yet the slightest twitch of one lip, the faintest glint of amusement in his eyes, left the impression that he was well aware Sir John's expressed delight was not sincere.

"Indeed, we are honoured," Lady Grandison said hurriedly. "And you must meet my goddaughter, Miss Cole. Harriet, Lord Sanderly."

Now his gaze really was on her, and she might have been back at the inn, dowdy, ragged, and vulnerable in a room full of amorous and entitled drunks. But absolutely no recognition dawned there. Stupidly piqued, she thrust out her hand.

"My lord."

If he was surprised, he gave no sign of that either. Unhurriedly, he took her hand in the very lightest and coolest of clasps and bowed. "Miss Cole."

She was released at once and wanted nothing more than to flee in the wake of her godmother who, however, did not move.

"And this is his lordship's sister, Lady Barbara Martindale," Lady Grandison said.

At first glance the brother and sister were not remotely alike. Interest and sheer vitality blazed out of Lady Barbara's pretty face. Her hair was dark brown rather than black, her eyes a paler shade of blue, but she smiled with genuine warmth as they touched hands.

"How do you do, Miss Cole?"

"Let us eat," Lady Grandison announced. "Sit where you will and make use of the terrace and the garden if you wish. I am glad there is no sign of yesterday's rain..."

"Shall we find a place to sit, Miss Cole?" Lady Barbara suggested. "Snake will bring us a first choice of morsels."

"I would," Sanderly drawled, "only I thought that was what husbands were for. Ladies."

He bowed and strolled off in the opposite direction to Lady Grandison, who was greeting other guests.

"How rude," someone said in a stage whisper behind them, though Lady Barbara did not seem remotely put out.

"Drat the man," she said without rancour, turning a brilliant smile on the gentleman who approached them. "He never used to be so disobliging. This is my husband, by the way, Mr. Martindale. James, meet Miss Cole, who is Lady Grandison's goddaughter."

Mr. Martindale was a stocky, somewhat austere looking gentleman, who, Harriet noted, had only approached once Sanderly had left them. Unlike his brother-in-law, he was both helpful and polite, escorted the ladies to a table on the terrace—as if they could not have tottered out there on their own—and immediately returned to the buffet table.

"We have not met before, have we?" Lady Barbara said in her friendly way. "Were you in London for the Season?"

"No, I have been at home with my family." Only home was no longer home. And she would not dwell on the pain of it. "To be honest, I have not been out much in society at all."

"Why is that?" asked Lady Barbara with unexpected directness.

"Mostly because my father died," Harriet said, brushing it aside. "Are you newly married, Lady Barbara?"

"Oh, call me Bab, everyone else does. And yes, we have only been married a few months. Am I not the luckiest lady alive?" She beamed as her husband emerged from the house bearing two loaded plates.

To Harriet, the man was well enough as appearance went, but there seemed nothing obvious to raise him from the ordinary, correct gentleman to the paragon so adored by his wife. He looked too serious for Harriet's taste. Clearly, she would have to know him better.

In fact, he proved to be pleasant company during luncheon, civil and friendly, and welcoming to Sir Ralph Lawrence who joined them later. Harriet gathered that they had all arrived at Grand Court yesterday and were well acquainted with each other.

"One is surprised to see Sanderly here," Sir Ralph remarked. "He is not known for gracing such parties."

"Oh, you know Snake," Bab said vaguely.

"Actually, I don't," Sir Ralph said. "He is somewhat...aloof."

Harriet was surreptitiously observing his lordship at the other side of the terrace, where he lounged in his peculiarly elegant manner opposite the lovely Mrs. Eldridge. Although a plate and a glass of wine stood before him, he appeared to be merely watching his companion eat, his eyes hooded by their heavy lids.

"Why do you call him Snake?" Harriet asked.

"Because he pounces like one," Mr. Martindale said.

"I gathered it was because he behaved like one," said a passing young matron with a tinkling laugh as she paused beside Lady Bab. "No offence, my dear, and all is fair in love and war, but he is not known for inspiring trust."

"*I* trust him," Bab said crossly. "And you are both wrong. The nickname was bestowed by our late brother Hugo when we were children. It's just a play on his Christian name."

"What is his Christian name?" Harriet asked. He looked somehow too distant to possess such an intimate thing.

Bab giggled. "Serpentine. Something to do with my parents walking in Hyde Park along the bank of the river when Mama informed Papa of the approaching happy event. Anyway, we thought it was funny, and the name stuck. I don't know why you all take it so seriously."

"Ask Alicia Eldridge," the matron said with a distinctly false smile and went on her way.

"Cat," murmured Bab.

Her husband pretended not to hear. "And will you be joining the pall-mall game this afternoon, Miss Cole?"

"If there is room for me on one of the teams, though I confess I have not played for some time."

"Oh, it is just for fun," Lady Bab touched her husband's hand. "No one takes it seriously, do they, James?"

"Probably not, since there is no money involved." He moved his hand to lift his wine glass.

Harriet noted that all the little looks and touches of affection between the married couple seemed to come from Bab. James was merely unfailingly polite.

"Cynical, Martindale," Sir Ralph said. "But we could arrange a little wager, if you are willing."

"Perhaps." Martindale was polite but not encouraging.

"Good God," said one apparently startled gentleman loudly, as he emerged from the garden room and stopped to stare. "Is that Snake Sanderly?"

The voice was sneering, dripping with contempt, and an uneasy silence descended upon the terrace. Everyone gazed avidly at the earl, as though awaiting a violent response. Sanderly's heavy eyelids rose and he regarded the newcomer without blinking, the full force of the icy blue orbs curiously hypnotic. Certainly, the young gentleman appeared unable to move or look away. The silence was tense.

"Ignore him," Lady Barbara breathed like a prayer.

At the door, the gentleman's sneering smile began to falter into blushing embarrassment. This was not the kind of attention he had sought and he clearly wished now that he'd kept his mouth shut.

"Hiss," Sanderly said.

For some reason, it was funny. Harriet let out a gurgle of laughter. The gentleman retreated back inside in some disorder, almost tripping over his surprised companions.

Bab giggled, and Sanderly returned to his contemplation of Mrs. Eldridge, saying something to her that produced low, musical laughter.

With difficulty, Harriet looked away, but the little scene disturbed her. Although Sanderly had turned it into comedy, the attitude of too many of her godmother's guests toward the earl smacked of bullying. Yet they seemed to regard such behaviour as justified. She contemplated this while the conversation went on around her.

"May I fetch you ladies something else?" Martindale asked.

"Oh, no, thank you, I am perfectly content," Harriet replied. She had not eaten so much for months, and her plates had all still been half full when she let the servant take them away.

"I believe I shall retire to my room and fortify myself for the afternoon's activity," Bab said. "James, why don't you reacquaint yourself with my brother?"

"Because he is busy with other reacquaintances," James said wryly. "I shall escort you instead."

They all rose to their feet. "I must go in search of Lady Grandison," Harriet said, somewhat mendaciously, and parted from her companions. What she really wanted was to walk off her luncheon at a brisk pace. She did not rule out running, so perhaps she should find the children. Deciding they were probably outdoors in the grounds somewhere, she set off to explore.

She found no sign of the children or anyone else in the formal, terraced garden, or the vast lawn laid out with pall-mall hoops. A nearby wood called to her, but she promised herself that treat in the morning. It had been so long since she had any free time not taken up with exhaustion that she felt almost guilty.

She should enjoy this time, for when she was a governess, she doubted she would have much freedom either.

Almost completing her circuit of the grounds immediately surrounding the house, she decided she felt marginally less full and should see how Lily fared before joining the pall-mall game. She wondered if the enigmatic Earl of Sanderly would play. Somehow, she could not imagine it, though she had a feeling it would be good for him.

At that point, just as she turned toward a side door in the house, a movement caught the corner of her eye, and she spun back to see the tall figure of a man vanishing through a gap in a high hedge.

It was as if she had conjured him up by her idle thought. *If* it was indeed Sanderly. She only glimpsed him for an instant and at some distance, but if she was right, then this was the perfect opportunity for her to speak to him alone and discharge her duty of gratitude. No doubt he would then apologise for his ill behaviour and the air would be cleared to begin afresh.

Begin what afresh? she wondered. She had no intention of going anywhere near him after this. They would merely be on polite nodding terms and that would be much more comfortable than this...whatever this was.

Harriet was a great believer in clearing the air, whether to mend or avoid quarrels. It had worked well for her in the past, simple honesty and the occasional apology invariably being met half-way, so that good humour and friendship were restored.

Except with Cousin Randolph, of course, who steadfastly refused to admit that he was in the wrong about anything, and insisted it was only his charity that kept their family together and solvent with a roof over their heads.

But Lord Sanderly was clearly not like that. Whatever anyone else said about him, he truly had done her and the children a good turn by giving up his comfortable room and he had expected nothing in return.

Still, she flitted across the grass at speed, eager to get the difficult moment over with before she lost courage. There was something extremely daunting about him, even if she ignored his insolent kiss.

Don't think of that! she admonished herself and whipped through the open gate of the high hedge, only to come to an abrupt halt. She was facing another tall hedge with only a narrow passage between it and the first. Various gaps opened off this second hedge. She was in a mature maze.

And there, lounging on a wrought-iron bench immediately to her left, his elegant arm draped casually along the back, was the Earl of Sanderly.

He looked right at her, those blazing blue eyes unshielded for the merest moment. It felt like being battered by...*something*. He did not immediately stand up, either from dismay or to give her time to flee. When she didn't take the opportunity, he unwound himself from the bench without hurry.

Mentally giving herself a short, sharp shake, she drew in her breath and dropped a curtsey. "Lord Sanderly."

"Miss Harriet Cole," he responded, with a bow that was surely ironic.

She held on to her determination, even took a step further into the maze to face him. "I am very glad to find you here, my lord."

"Flattered as I am, I came here for solitude."

Although it was unforgivably rude of him, Harriet understood the sentiment and said at once, "Don't worry, I shall keep you a mere moment."

He blinked, which may have been a sign of surprise. At any rate, his heavy eyelids drooped further, hiding the startling beauty of those amazing eyes.

Harriet hurried into her speech. "I have to thank you for your kindness in giving up your room at the inn to us. It was the only safety possible for my family and me, and we are all grateful."

Now, she thought, her tension reaching agonizing levels, *he will apologize, and we can part and be comfortable and never speak of this again...*

"My dear girl," he drawled, "there was no kindness involved. I fully expected payment for my key, only the dice distracted me."

It was a lie.

She knew that instinctively, even if she didn't understand the reason behind it. "Yes, yes, but since you did not receive it, we shall agree I have cause to be grateful."

"Indubitably," he said, amusement creeping into his soft voice. He even prowled toward her, "Only...how grateful?"

"Don't start that again," Harriet said severely, although she took a circumspect step backward. "We both made a mistake at the inn. I have acknowledged mine—"

"And I mine," he said provokingly. "Never choose dice over women."

"That was not your mistake and we are both well aware of it!"

"My little innocent," he mocked, still advancing. "There are so many opportunities for dalliance at such parties as this, but discretion is the watchword, darling. Next time, let me come to you."

Pride and outrage warred with sense, especially when he halted so close he was almost touching. She could feel his breath on her upturned face, smell his rather tantalizing scent of warm male skin and soap. Somewhere wicked and deep inside her, she wondered if the same incomprehensible dizziness would overcome her if he kissed her again. But he was right about one thing. Discretion *was* the watchword, and in this particular situation, it was quite definitely the better part of valour.

She stepped back again, whirling toward the gate.

"Don't be ridiculous," she flung over her shoulder, a mere sop to her pride, and fled.

HAD HARRIET BEEN PRIVY to Sanderly's thoughts, she might well have felt less routed. In truth, he had made his final move and had no intention of going any further, even for another taste of her strangely sweet lips. So he had reached an impasse with no idea what to do next, except verbally blister her, which he was inexplicably reluctant to do.

Her sudden flight was therefore a relief to him, requiring him to do no more than sink back on his solitary bench and smile gently to himself where no one could see.

He had to admit the dowdy girl in the battered straw hat scrubbed up damned well. Without doubt, she would put the cat amongst the pigeons at this party, casting both debutantes and the most beautiful of worldly young matrons into the shade. Perhaps he should stay another day to watch it happen.

He had already agreed to stay at Grand Court until tomorrow in order to sort out Bab's mess with Illsworth and her dull husband. His ship sailed with tomorrow's early tide, with or without him. But as Bab pointed out, there were other ships.

On the other hand, did he really want to spend more time than he already had among these tedious, self-righteous members of the ton? No, Africa called him with its intensity of life and colour, its vast, unexplored lands, populated with very different peoples and much more dangerous animals than the odd lapdog or mouse-catching cat. For Sanderly, rightly or wrongly, Africa had come to represent relief and freedom and rebirth. He longed for that.

And yet he was allowing himself to be distracted by his sister's trivial problems that she had undoubtedly brought upon herself. And by the intriguing girl whose battered straw hat was probably being burned even now in her godmother's furnace.

He supposed he understood about creating one's own problems. No doubt it was a family failing. As for the girl, Miss Harriet Cole, he owed her nothing. Much more available and interesting women were ten-a-penny in his experience. So why he should feel the faintest urge to protect this one was beyond him.

Halfway through his yawn, he realized the answer.

When she had come across him before luncheon, she had smiled right at him, as though genuinely pleased to see him. At the inn, she had laughed at a sally which anyone else would have understood as insulting. She had done the same during the encounter with that puppy, Dolt, on the terrace. The silly girl seemed to *like* him.

She did not crave his favours, his bed, his shock-value, or his title. She gave him the benefit of the doubt when no one else ever had, even enduring considerably more provocation. She had even pursued him here to seek some kind of rapprochement.

Well, that won't last, he thought cynically. *I give her until tea to turn against me.*

He closed his eyes, listening to the songs of the birds and the buzzing of distant insects, inhaling the sweet smells and the sunshine of summer. Until distant, human voices began to intrude and he supposed it was time for a tedious and no doubt flirtatious game of pall-mall.

What a pity he had to ignore Miss Harriet Cole.

Chapter Six

Sanderly was aware of the moment Cedric Illsworth arrived at Grand Court, for the man had one of those loud, penetrating voices that set one's teeth on edge.

Sanderly had already played his obligatory game of pall-mall. He had repressed his urge to whack the ball hard enough to lift the hoops off the ground, and was now stretched out on a bench in the sun, pretending to be asleep while he amused himself observing Harriet Cole.

She was oddly joyous in her game, as though nothing had ever been so much fun. He wondered about her past, while admiring her focus and her slender shape, and smiling inwardly at her frequent laughter.

Illsworth's much more strident tones could be heard at the front of the house. Sanderly could almost feel Bab's glare as she willed Sanderly to immediately go about her business. Sanderly, however, had no intention of appearing so eager. Bab had no subtlety, which was how she had got into this mess in the first place.

Illsworth did not join them in the pall-mall games. Sanderly presumed he planned to make an entrance at tea, or perhaps supper. There was no sign of Wolf either, who was presumably nursing a hangover of mammoth proportions. Perhaps Illsworth did too.

Sanderly allowed himself to yawn and stretch, then strolled unhurriedly away from the pall-mall players toward the house. He ignored his sister.

Entering by the garden room, he found it empty, although as he passed through, he could hear the sounds of childish hilarity in the room next door.

"Go on, Harry, bash it down the line!" urged a boy's gleeful voice.

On impulse, Sanderly turned away from the staircase and sauntered into the next room instead. Three somewhat ill-dressed children—a boy and two girls—of various sizes were jumping up and down by the window. Although Sanderly had barely glimpsed them at the Duck and Spoon, he was quite sure who they were.

Poor Lady Grandison, he thought with some amusement, as they cheered and then grumbled as, presumably, "Harry" missed the hoop.

"Drat it," said the taller girl. "Now that old fellow will win."

"But the old have so little to look forward to," Sanderly said sardonically. "It is a kindness to let old Thornton win something."

They all turned to him in surprise. Oh yes, they were Harriet's siblings. They all had a similar, direct gaze and quick smile, the same-shaped noses and pointed chins, even though the shades of their hair were lighter and straighter in two cases.

"Do you think so, sir?" the girl said in some surprise. "I think he has just practised a lot and likes beating the younger folk to flinders."

"And Harriet, you know, has not played for years," the boy said.

"Why is that?" Sanderly asked, sauntering across to the window from where there was a fine view of the game.

"Randolph," the small girl said with loathing. The others nudged her. She glared up at them. "Well, he *is* awful!"

"Is he?" Sanderly wondered.

"Yes," said the larger girl. "Very awful, but we don't mean to speak of him."

"Well, I am pretty awful myself," Sanderly said, "so you needn't mind speaking of him to me. You are Miss Cole's siblings?"

"Yes," said the girls.

"No," said the boy. "I'm a cousin."

"Randolph wants to 'prentice him instead of sending him to school," said the little one, shifting agilely aside to avoid the inevitable buffets. "I expect you agree, if you're as awful as Randolph."

The refined accents and the early bolting from the Duck and Spoon began to make some kind of sense. "Are you running away from Randolph?" he inquired.

"No!" the older girl said, glaring at her sister. "We have accepted an invitation to stay with Harriet's godmother. Who is Lady Grandison."

"Very wise."

The children were regarding him with more favour again. Except for the little girl who said uneasily, "You don't know Randolph, do you?"

"Oh, no. At least I hope not. We awful people tend to keep as much distance as possible between us. My name is Sanderly."

"How do you do, Mr. Sanderly," said the boy politely. He bowed, as did the little girl. The older girl gave a reluctant curtsey.

"How do you do?" Sanderly replied affably, "though I must correct myself. More properly, Sanderly is my title. My name is Fforbes. With two Fs," he added.

"Why are there two Fs?" the little one demanded.

"Who knows? In case I lose one, I expect."

The boy grinned. The girls giggled. The older girl said, "I'm Rose Cole. This is my sister Orchid, and my cousin is Alex."

"Delighted to make your acquaintance."

"Yes, but what do we call you?" Alex asked.

Sanderly considered. "Snake," he said. "Except in public, when I suppose you should call me my lord. But do tell me how the awful Randolph stopped Miss Harriet from playing pall-mall?"

The subsequent conversation was enlightening. He endeared himself to the children further by commenting that it sounded as if the unspeakable Randolph needed a punch on the nose.

Alex grinned. "Draw his cork, sir! I say, were you at the prize fight yesterday?"

The girls groaned, just as a maid bustled into the room. "*There* you are, children! It's tea time."

"Can we have it with Lily in her bedchamber?" Orchid asked. "Lily isn't well," she added to Sanderly. "She's our other sister and she's staying in Harriet's room until she's better."

"Stop bothering the gentleman and come away," the nursemaid said hastily.

They went obediently enough, although they cast conspiratorial grins over their shoulders at him. They were really very like Harriet, smiling still, although the whole family was clearly escaping from an entirely unacceptable situation. He could guess some, at least, of what had not been said.

None of your business, Sanderly. He always referred to himself as Sanderly, even in his thoughts, something he had forced himself to do when Hugo died. It still felt unnatural and utterly wrong, but at least his whole being no longer contracted in pain.

No, it was none of his business. But he wished them well in their escape.

"YOU REALLY DON'T MIND about the Coles being here?" Lady Grandison said to her husband as she changed for dinner. Sir John, resplendent in evening dress, complete with a "waterfall" arrangement of his cravat, and a gold, crested pin that matched his sleeve buttons, had wandered into her dressing room while the maid was putting the finishing touches to her coiffure.

Sir John took a pinch of snuff and closed the box. "Of course not, my love, except in so far as it makes additional work for you."

"More for the servants," she admitted. "I've brought the seamstress up from the village, but even so, a couple of the maids are necessary to help with all the sewing—there are the children to think of as well as Harriet, because I really can't have them *seen*, even in the grounds in those disgusting rags."

"A little overstated, my dear," Sir John said mildly. "Ill-fitting and excessively mended, but they do not wear *rags*."

"Not quite, but John, what is Randolph Cole thinking to let them go about so? Keeping them virtually prisoners in their own home..."

"Well, that's the thing. It is not their home any longer. It is Randolph's. He is not obliged to keep them at all. Arguably, he is saving their trust funds."

"By using Harriet as a servant when she should be going to parties and finding a husband? The girl is an heiress of means and as pretty as a picture. Why isn't he using that to get them all off his hands? I wonder if you shouldn't post up to Gorsefield to call on him, bring him to his senses? After the party, of course."

"Whenever I go, I have no rights in the matter. I am quite content to house them all at Grand Court. But have you considered, my dear? We will need governesses and tutors, and Alex should probably go away to school at some point."

"Harriet has a plan," Lady Grandison said with a sigh. "She has applied for a post as governess, which she is convinced she will be given, and from her salary, she thinks to send them all to school so that they only need join us for occasional holidays. She has no idea of the costs!"

Sir John sat on the chaise longue. "I imagine Harriet would be a breath of fresh air as a governess and whoever she taught would adore her. On the other hand, I can't actually imagine anyone employing her. She is far too young and much too irreverent."

Lady Grandison rose, her eyes sparkling. "Exactly! But I have a better plan. Marriage!" she finished in triumph.

"With whom?" he asked warily.

"We have lots of eligible bachelors here! Sir Ralph is already very taken with her, but he is not the only one. There is Dolt and Fool."

"My dear!" Sir John protested.

"Well, the nicknames are unkind. They merely need to grow up a little. Neither of them would be my first choice but they are both of excellent birth and fortune. Lord Wolf would be better for her, though I suspect his pockets are to let."

"His pockets are full of holes," Sir John said dryly.

"True, but I always had a soft spot for him. But there is no point in my choosing for her. Harriet is like her dear mama and will select her own husband. I just have to ensure she has a wide choice, and she does! I might hint that her fortune is a little larger than it is..."

"And whoever she chooses will find out."

"Well, if he's worthy of her, he won't care. Of course I shan't be vulgar about it. Indeed I shall be very vague."

"With what aim?" Sir John asked, mystified.

"Just to boost her popularity. You know what men are. They value something or someone—much more if it is coveted by others."

"Some men, perhaps."

She dropped a kiss on the top of his head. "Not you, of course, dear, but others."

"Like Wriggley? Illsworth? Sanderly?"

"Oh, I think I draw the line at Sanderly, dear. I don't want her *ostracized*."

"To be honest, I'm surprised you invited him."

"I didn't think he'd come," she admitted. "Everyone said he was fleeing the country, and in any case, he never accepts invitations. It was Bab who summoned him, suddenly panicking, no doubt, that she would never see him again."

"I would have thought she'd thank God, fasting."

"Oh, no. She never speaks ill of him, if you notice. As a result, people rarely do so in front of her—at least no one with any honour or kindness. So she doesn't really know half of what is said about him." She frowned suddenly. "And only a quarter of that can possibly be true. He is his own worst enemy, is Sanderly, but decidedly he will not do for Harriet. Shall we go down, Sir John?"

Obediently, he rose and offered his arm. "Be discreet, my love. Don't tell everyone poor Harriet's as rich as a nabob."

"All these years, Sir John, and you still doubt my subtlety…"

DRESSED EARLY FOR DINNER, Sanderly made his way purposefully along the empty passage to Illsworth's room. He had found no chance to beard the miscreant either before, during or after tea, for Illsworth, like everyone else, avoided him.

Martindale—dear James—was also keeping well out of his way.

Nevertheless, Sanderly had hopes of being in Harwich by the morrow. If he got the wretched cravat pin back now, then he could lecture James over the after-dinner port when he was likely to be more susceptible. Then his duty to his sister would be done and he could escape. He could find passage on another ship, if his own had already sailed, which seemed increasingly likely.

But he would be free.

He paused an instant at Illsworth's door. The footman at the end of the hall—whom he had bribed for the information—gave the faintest of nods. Sanderly's lips twisted of their own accord. He gave a brief, faint knock and immediately sauntered into the room.

Illsworth stood before a looking glass in his shirt sleeves, wrestling with his cravat. His startled gaze met Sanderly's in the glass.

"Illsworth," Sanderly said fondly, as if they had just run into each other by accident. "How do you do?"

"Struggling, if you want the truth. I wish I had not left my man in town. It seemed such a good idea not to have his disapproving face around when I went to watch the fight, but now, as you see…"

"I do," Sanderly said, eyeing the mess of the other man's cravat. "Still, never mind, the pin is the thing. Is it not?"

Illsworth understood. It was in his eyes, a hint of surprise and irritation before he smiled as blandly as ever. "Not to me, Sanderly. My man has a way with the folds of the cravat. I don't suppose I could borrow your fellow?"

"Sadly not. He gave notice rather than brave foreign shores. Allow me."

Illsworth tried to whip off the necktie, but Sanderly was faster, quickly adjusting the folds. Illsworth's hands fell to his sides, clenched tight. His body was rigid as Sanderly created order of the mess the other man had created.

"There," Sanderly said, holding out one hand, palm upward, while continuing to hold the cravat in place with the other. "Pin."

There was a pause. If Illsworth hadn't guessed his purpose before, he definitely knew now. He moved, picking something off the dressing table and dropped it into Sanderly's palm.

Sanderly had little idea what Bab's pin had looked like beyond the fact it contained a sapphire. But it was certainly not jet. "Not that one. Too severe." He met Illsworth's gaze. "Or not severe enough. Either way, it is quite wrong. You promised my sister you would wear the one she gave you."

Illsworth's eyes all but dripped with contempt. "If I had such a thing, I would not put it in your hand."

Sanderly gave his most unpleasant smile, the one which had once reduced subalterns and the most recalcitrant of private soldiers to instant obedience, and which nowadays made society shudder.

"Is that honour you are pretending? Better late than never. My sister asked you to return the pin. You will do so now."

"She is not here," Illsworth sneered, "whatever scandal you may have heard about her. Feel free to look."

Sanderly sighed. "Don't try my patience, Illsworth."

Illsworth laughed. "Or what, *Snake*? You'll call me out? The officer cashiered for cowardice?"

"Of course I won't call you out," Sanderly said softly. The world would guess why, which would be disastrous for Bab. "But never rely on any man's cowardice, certainly not when his fingers are at your throat." He changed his grip on the cravat, crushing it and twisting it tight.

Instinctively, Illsworth grabbed at his wrist, tugging. Sanderly twisted harder.

"The pin, if you please."

Illsworth began to struggle in earnest, using both hands to try and push him off, but he fought as though he were young Alex's age, which was interesting.

"Don't make an enemy of me, Illsworth," Sanderly said softly. "Just give me the pin."

"I don't know what you're talking about!" Illsworth gasped.

Sanderly gave another vicious twist.

"I haven't got it!" Illsworth croaked, when Sanderly loosened the necktie enough for him to do so. "It was stolen from me! Look!"

He grasped a box on the dressing table which contained two pairs of sleeve buttons and one cravat pin beside the one Sanderly had discarded. It was plain gold.

Sanderly looked from the box back to Illsworth. The man could be lying. But there was just enough outrage in his voice to be convincing.

Sanderly let go of the necktie and Illsworth staggered back into the mirror.

"When was it stolen?" he demanded.

"I don't know," Illsworth gasped, tugging the necktie loose from his throat. "At the Duck and Spoon, probably. No doubt by that girl you tumbled. No wonder she was so damned grateful. I'd check your own possessions."

Sanderly had no intention of drawing the man's attention to the fact that the girl in question was now at Grand Court. He simply said, "When did you last see it?"

"When I packed it—when my man packed it—in London."

"And when did you notice it was gone?"

Illsworth shrugged impatiently, though his eyes slid free. "Just now."

So the weasel *had* been about to wear it this evening. Sanderly curled his lip and looked Illsworth up and down. "And people wonder why I eschew society."

Since there was nothing more to be gained here, he strode to the door without a word of farewell. He had grasped the handle before Illsworth sneered. "And no one eschews you, Snake?"

"Oh, it is undoubtedly mutual," Sanderly agreed with some amusement. Illsworth actually seemed to think it was a barb. If it ever had been, it had ceased to prick a long time ago.

He emerged into the passage, by ill fortune, just as James Martindale strode past. He wore evening dress, but he did not have his wife on his arm. Sanderly, fully expecting to be ignored again, paused to give an elaborate bow.

Unexpectedly, James halted, glaring at him. "I might have known why you reared your damned head here. Stirring the pot as usual! Playing Cupid, Sanderly?"

"Good God, no. You of all people should know that the liaisons of others revolt me."

"Then what are you doing with *him*?"

"Well, if you lower your voice and show any sense I might tell you," Sanderly said, turning back along the passage in the opposite direction. "Discretion, dear James, is the thing. Bab still in her room?"

He didn't wait for an answer, which was fortunate, since James never gave him one.

He found Bab in her bedchamber, being presented with a fan and reticule by her maid, whom he dismissed with a single jerk of his head. The woman fled with the barest scared glance at her mistress.

"Snake!" Bab pounced. "Have you got it? Did he at least promise not to wear it in front of James?"

"No. And no. And you have just removed my last suspicion that you got it back yourself. He says it was stolen, somewhere between London and Grand Court."

Bab stared at him. "And you believe him?"

"Mostly, yes."

She sank into the chair behind her. "But who would have done such a thing? If he reports it to Lady Grandison, there will be all sorts of unpleasantness and if it is found..."

"Exactly." He found himself frowning at his sister. "The man's a rat, Bab."

"I know," she whispered. "I thought he was a friend."

"No one has any friends in a tight corner."

Unexpectedly, her eyes cleared. "You do, you know, Snake. You should just stop pushing them away. Come, you may escort me down to dinner since James was in such a wretched hurry. Have you spoken to him yet?"

"He's my after dinner treat," Sanderly drawled.

Chapter Seven

Lady Grandison's people had worked another miracle, providing Harriet with a startlingly lovely evening dress of pastel green gauze over a white silk slip. Her ladyship lent her "my old emeralds" to wear with it. The jewels should have overwhelmed both Harriet and the pale gown, yet somehow did not.

"They unite everything and draw attention to your eyes and your face," Rose pronounced. "And I have to say, Harry you look lovely."

Orchid nodded with rather more doubt. "Yes, but you still don't look like Harry."

"Yes, she does," Lily said from the bed, where she had wakened up for the viewing. "More like she used to look."

This comment seemed to reassure Orchid, who took Harriet's hand to escort her to the bedchamber door, while the others trooped after them, and Harriet made sure they would nag Lily to drink her willow bark tea before she fell asleep again. In fact, although Lily smiled and lifted a hand to wave her off, the girl's sleepiness worried her. She had done little but sleep since they had left the inn this morning. Fortunately, the fever seemed to have receded, but surely no one should sleep quite so much?

It was only as she entered the blue salon, where the guests gathered before dinner, that she was distracted from anxiety by the realization that she was alone and being gawped at by everyone in the room.

A thousand trivial fears paralyzed her. Had her hair come loose? Had the children played some trick that she hadn't noticed and smeared something on her face or her gown? Had Orchid left a muddy footprint on the hem?

Then it came to her with a jolt. Several of the staring faces belonged to the drunken gentlemen form the inn. The two who had dared touch her, two others who had been sitting with Lord Sanderly. They had all seen her enter alone. They had all seen Sanderly kiss her and watched her follow the innkeeper's wife to his room. Why had she not thought of this before? Why had she not seen or recognized—

"There you are!" It was Sir John who rescued her, presenting her with his arm and a small glass of sherry. She grasped both like lifelines, and the conversation started up again. "Don't mind the staring," Sir John said kindly. "Your beauty has drawn all eyes, and no wonder."

"I wondered if I had a smut on my nose."

Sir John laughed. "It's admiration you see, not criticism. Eliza has placed you with Sir Ralph for dinner."

This was a relief, since Sir Ralph had not been at the Duck and Spoon. She wondered how long it would take chatter about her to reach the ears of the Grandisons. Would they throw the children out along with her? Why had she not told her godmother about the incident at the inn? Because she was trying not to dwell upon it, and it had never entered her head she would encounter such scoundrels here...

Somehow, she got through the ordeal of dinner. The sherry and the wine helped. So did Sir Ralph, of the ready smile and the sad eyes, who made conversation that was both distracting and interesting. To her horror, a gentleman who had been at the inn was placed on her other side. He was apparently Lord Illsworth, who had been playing hazard with Sanderly. But if he recognized her, he gave no sign of it, making merely pleasant conversation with her when he was not devoting his time to Lady Barbara Martindale on his other side. She rather thought he did not really *see* most people, being too absorbed in himself.

Almost directly opposite her was Sanderly himself. As far as she could tell, he never so much as glanced at her throughout, but then she barely looked anywhere other than her food or the gentlemen on either side of her.

Harriet was quite relieved when at long last Lady Grandison rose to lead the ladies out to the drawing room. Only then she wondered if the gossip had reached the women too and if they would shun her. Mrs. Eldridge certainly sailed past her without acknowledgement, though immediately afterward, Bab Martindale caught up with her.

Taking her courage in both hands, Harriet resolved to find out the truth. "I don't believe Mrs. Eldridge likes me," she murmured low to Bab.

"Oh it's me she doesn't like," Bab said carelessly. "She's afraid I know my brother has—er... moved on. To be fair, I suppose it's not very flattering to think one's lover is fleeing to Africa to escape one."

"Oh," Harriet said weakly, trying not to look shocked. "Is he?"

"Escaping the lot of us, I should think, but I might have caused him to miss the boat, and that can only be a good thing. Or do you mean, is he her lover? Not anymore and he never goes back. And I shouldn't be gossiping so scandalously with an unmarried young lady. You are far too easy to confide in, and now you must forget I spoke."

That, of course was impossible, but it was her own scandals rather than Sanderly's she wished to discuss with Bab. To her embarrassment, one of the young gentlemen from the inn held the dining room door for them and cast Harriet a far too intimate smile as she passed through.

She must have looked outraged or frightened or both, for Bab said. "Don't mind Dolt. He's an inveterate fortune hunter."

"But I don't have a fortune."

"Don't you?" Bab said vaguely.

"Well, it's not vast and it's not mine until I'm five-and-twenty."

"Or married, I daresay," Bab guessed.

"Yes, but I won't be."

"Then prepare to repel the besiegers. But marriage is fun, you know." The smile died in her eyes and then on her lips. "Or at least it used to be," she said, almost beneath her breath.

"Would you like to go to the cloakroom before joining the others?" asked Harriet, distracted from her own troubles.

"I'd rather go for a walk."

"So would I. Do you need a shawl?"

"No, I need the fresh air."

So did Harriet. Veering toward the staircase, they slipped away and out of the garden room door. Although darkness had fallen, there was enough light from the hanging lanterns and from the moon to make out the terrace and the garden paths.

"If something troubles you, I will try to help," Harriet said at last. "But equally, I shall not be offended if you would rather I minded my own business. My siblings choose either course, depending on their mood."

Bab took her arm. "You must be an excellent sister. I am a poor one, and a worse wife."

"I'm sure that is not true."

"Oh, it's quite true. I let Hugo die, I ignore Snake though I don't want him to leave, and in less than six months, I have turned my husband's adoration to indifference."

Harriet wanted to ask about her brothers but, suspecting this was not the subject currently disturbing her most, she said instead, "I am sure your husband still adores you."

"Then you have not really looked. Though, of course, you never saw him before when he loved me. He was attentive and spent time with me, spoke of love and brought me flowers… A hundred little gestures of affection every day that I took for granted."

Harriet considered. "Perhaps one cannot keep up that level of outward devotion. It does not mean it isn't there inside." All the same, she had already noted Martindale avoided her touch and, while perfectly civil in his attentions, he did not linger or escort her anywhere unless she demanded it aloud.

"I do not care about those outward things. I care that his eyes are cold, that he never smiles at me, that he does not..." She broke off, blushing and issuing a choked little laugh. "Drat you, Harriet, why do you always have me speaking so improperly? How old are you?"

"Nineteen."

"So am I. Snake didn't want me to marry James."

"Who did he want you to marry?"

Bab blinked. "No one. He just thought James would bore me. Neither of us suspected I would bore him."

"Lady Bab, he is not bored. He is...that is, he looks to me like...a...a schoolboy in a miff. I don't believe he is remotely indifferent."

"Do you think not?" Bab said eagerly. "The thing is, I am a trying person to live with, and I act before I think, which is how I came to flirt with another and even give him..." She trailed off sighing. "And that is another thing. In a moment of spite, instantly regretted, I gave him a cravat pin James had given me, a love token that I wore as a brooch, which I should never have parted with. Anyway, Ills... this man would not give it back. Now I'm sure James notices I no longer wear it and Ill—er... the man I gave it to claims it was stolen from him and he can't return it."

"Do you believe him?" Harriet asked when she had disentangled the threads of this.

"Not entirely, but I can't exactly search his room for the wretched thing."

"Why not?" Harriet asked.

Bab's lips twitched upward. "I knew I would like you. Because if I was discovered in his room by anyone at all, the scandal would spread instantly to James, and I would be utterly undone."

"Yes, I see." Harriet nodded. "Whereas, I am a silly newcomer who might easily have wandered into the wrong room."

"But that is even worse since you are unmarried!"

"Oh, I am going away soon in any case, but it would only be gossip rather than true scandal if I did it while he is in the company of everyone else. Let me think... What does this cravat pin look like?"

WHEN THE LADIES HAD withdrawn from the dining room and the port and brandy were being passed freely among the gentlemen, Sanderly was glad to discover that Grandison was an informal host. Remarks and jests flew up and down and across the table; men moved seats to avoid shouting and to enjoy deeper conversations. Still, the time would be limited, for Grandison would not wish to take a bunch of inebriates into his wife's drawing room. Sanderly would have to act quickly, considering the presence of Wriggley, Dolt, and Fool...to say nothing of the newly arrived Wolf, who seemed to be knocking back the brandy with more than usual abandon.

Martindale—dear James—could make pleasant conversation with the best of the ton, but he shone more in formal situations, too concerned, perhaps, with his own dignity—although to be fair, Sanderly's assessment sprang from the few occasions they had been forced to meet in each other's houses, including the wedding breakfast. Sanderly rarely went to clubs or to society parties except to escort Bab before her marriage when he couldn't rope in uncles or cousins to take his place. He preferred the Sanderly estates, only since his return from the Peninsula, the English sun seemed too pale, the colours of the countryside too bland.

When had lush green become duller than parched earth?

Stick to the matter in hand, he told himself severely. He sat somewhat aloofly in the midst of the amiable chatter. Grandison made occasional efforts to draw him into conversation, and he murmured a few words just to be polite. He was well aware people only listened in case he said anything outrageously cutting or shocking enough to pass on as gossip.

But Sanderly had no quarrel with Grandison. He had been perfectly decent about his unwelcome descent upon his party, and he appeared to have accepted the entire Cole brood in the same amiable spirit of hospitality.

Sir John rose and moved around the table to speak to Thornton and Illsworth. Sanderly twisted the stem of his brandy glass between his fingers and regarded James. There were a few vacant seats to his left. Dolt, on his right, was his nearest neighbour at the moment, but Sanderly knew how to scare him off.

Rising with his glass, he strolled around the table and took the empty chair between James and Dolt. Inevitably, Dolt looked outraged before deliberately rising and going to join his friend Fool who seemed to be annoying Wolf at the other side of the table.

"James," Sanderly said fondly.

To give him his due, James seemed neither alarmed nor irritated. On the other hand, no one could have interpreted his expression as pleased to see his brother-in-law so close.

"Sanderly," James responded.

"Indeed. I have—er... *reared my damned head* once more."

Recognizing his own less than gracious words, James had the grace to blush. He shifted in his seat. "I apologize for my temper earlier. I spoke in haste and much too rudely."

"Oh, be as rude as you like," Sanderly encouraged. "You are family, after all. It is the cross you took up by marrying my sister."

James regarded him with a hint of suspicion, but interestingly, no fear. Most people regarded Sanderly with fear, either of his sharp tongue or the social damage caused by being seen with him. Now that he thought of it, he had never surprised that look in James's eyes.

The man frowned but clearly struggled for a reply.

"You do remember my sister, don't you?" Sanderly prompted.

"Of course I remember my own wife! And I am well aware you were always against the match."

"Not always. I seem to recall consenting and, in fact, I—er... gave you her hand in St. George's, Hanover Square."

"Then your memory is as good as mine," James retorted.

"Better, it seems. You appear to have forgotten why you married Bab despite her obnoxious relation. And why she fought tooth and nail to be allowed to marry you. And she did, you know."

Involuntarily, James's eyes strayed across the table to Illsworth, who was rather too carefully avoiding glancing in their direction while he listened to Grandison and Thornton.

Sanderly sighed. "You knew when you married her that she was a flirt by nature. You assured me you recognized the true value of the woman beneath. That is what you have forgotten. She may flirt still, but she remains the same woman beneath. Loyal and true, as they say. If you don't know that, then you never deserved her."

From blushing, James seemed to have paled, though it might have been the fault of the candlelight. "Proving you right to refuse my suit in the first place?"

"Only think how everyone would hate that. What did you imagine she would do after a quarrel? Go into a decline until you forgave her? No, she flirted with the first man she saw to make you jealous. And by God, it worked, though not quite in the way she meant. Allow me to call you a complete gudgeon."

James opened his mouth, but Sanderly had not finished.

"Make yourself miserable by all means, James. But be assured, I won't tolerate your doing the same to my sister." He smiled and rose once more, raising his glass very slightly to his brother-in-law. "Dear James. Always a pleasure to talk to you."

LILY WAS ASLEEP WHEN Harriet looked in on her, but since she was not fevered, Harriet felt no compunction in removing the younger children and negotiating a reasonable bed time with Mildred the nursery maid. She only made it to the drawing room a few minutes before the gentlemen joined the ladies.

So that Illsworth would suspect no collusion between them, Harriet sat well away from Bab, settling instead beside her godmother, who demanded an update on Lily's health.

Naturally, the arrival of the gentlemen changed everything. The debutantes sat straighter and began to sparkle, whether on their own initiative or prodded—literally—by their mothers.

Mrs. Eldridge and the young matrons were much too sophisticated to be so obvious, but Harriet was sure she knew who was involved with whom. Mrs. Eldridge flicked open her fan and smiled at no one in particular, although her face always seemed to be pointed toward Sanderly. Mrs. Archer, the beauty who had spoken ill of Sanderly at luncheon, made space on her sofa for Lord Wolf—another dice player from the inn.

Bab's face lit up at sight of her husband who, Harriet was relieved to see, went straight to her. Perhaps he had realized how much his wife truly loved him. So if only she could extract the cravat pin from Illsworth, all should be well.

Such were Harriet's thoughts when she saw with some alarm that several gentlemen were all but charging toward *her*. And just when Lady Grandison took it into her head to move across the room.

Worse, two of the men at the front had been at the Duck and Spoon.

"Miss Cole," the first said breathlessly, bowing and hurling himself into Lady Grandison's vacated chair. "What an unexpected joy to find you alone."

"Hardly," Harriet murmured, watching in bewilderment as another man inserted himself between them, settling on the arm of the first gentleman's chair. Another moved a hard backed chair to sit directly opposite her, an action quickly copied by a fourth.

Was this to be a repeat of the mob-insult at the Duck and Spoon? Surely they would not dare in such surroundings, when she was under the Grandisons' protection?

Involuntarily, her gaze sought out Lord Sanderly, lounging alone on the window seat. Impossible to tell if his eyes were open, let alone where they might be focused.

"You know, I can't help feeling we have met before, ma'am," said the first man, leaning forward to address her around his friend. "Perhaps it was at Almack's?"

"No, sir, I have never been to London."

"What, never?" asked the chair arm man in astonishment.

Were they making fun of her?

"Never," she said flatly. "You'll forgive me gentlemen, but I have met so many new people since arriving at Grand Court, that I have completely forgotten your names."

"Allow me to present Dolt and Fool," said the man opposite her with some malice.

"My name is Dolton," the first man said, sparing him a glare before indicating the chair arm man. "And this is Mr. Poole. Some people rejoice in rude and childish nicknames."

"I am sure they are mere joking nicknames," Harriet said.

"Hardly, when Snake Sanderly gave them," said the man opposite with some amusement.

Harriet recalled that Dolton had, in fact, been the man who had tried to humiliate Sanderly at luncheon and been routed. She supposed the contemptuous nicknames made sense of that.

"No one pays any attention to *him*," Dolt muttered.

"And yet the names have stuck," said the fourth man, leaning forward. "Bennett Wriggley, Miss Cole, at your service."

"How do you do?" Harriet said politely.

"Why, I am well and deliriously happy to be in your company."

Harriet regarded him quite carefully, but he was not even joking. He had been at the inn, like Dolt and Fool—*Dolton and Poole*!—but as far as she could tell, none of them recognized her. Of course they had been drunk as wheelbarrows, which might just have saved her reputation, but the question remained, what were they about now?

For the next ten minutes, they competed to pay her fulsome compliments, to make her laugh, to ensure her comfort by fetching shawls or cushions, and to secure dances at tomorrow evening's waltzing party and at the upcoming Grand ball next week. Once she stopped worrying, she found them mildly amusing, although she was in no danger of believing a word. No doubt she was the point of some wager, or just a contest she could not understand. Of course it did nothing to endear her to the other debutantes.

As planned, when the tea trolley was wheeled in and placed in front of Lady Grandison, Bab rose, ferried a cup of tea to her husband, and then sauntered away to sit by a small group who included Lord Illsworth. James's eyes hardened once more, and Harriet wished ruefully that they had thought of another way of keeping Illsworth in sight. Well, it was not as if Bab was engaging in a tête-à-tête with the man.

As soon as Harriet rose, the men around her sprang up too, causing rather more of a stir than she would have liked. Especially as, when she murmured, "Excuse me, gentlemen," a fifth seemed to materialize from nowhere asking if he could fetch her a cup of tea.

"Oh, no thank you, not at this moment. I just have to..."

"Allow me to escort you, Miss Cole."

This was getting ridiculous. She looked him in the eye. "Thank you, no," she said firmly. As she had hoped, he blushed, grasping that he could not escort her to the cloakroom.

Past that obstacle, she had to veer off course to avoid another man advancing purposefully toward her and then all but sprint to the drawing room door, smothering a slightly hysterical urge to laugh. Her exit had hardly been the discreet departure she and Bab had planned, but at least no one was following her.

And there, peering over the banister, were Alex and Orchid. They grinned at her and she hurried toward them, as if that had always been her plan. The footmen below may have wondered why, after a quick exchange of words, she did not sweep them upstairs with her, but left them where they were while she hurried up to the landing. Rose, lurking there with a doll and a vast array of clothes for it, winked at her.

Harriet winked back. "Pay attention," she murmured, and turned not right toward the family rooms where she was quartered but left toward the guest rooms.

Fortunately, the footmen could not have seen that. She would just have to watch out now for maids and valets.

She counted along the doors according to Bab's instructions, hoping fervently that they were accurate. She paused an instant outside what she hoped was Illsworth's room and glanced both ways along the empty passage before trying the door.

It was not locked. Which either meant he had nothing to hide or he was careless. She slipped inside and closed the door. A lamp, turned low, burned on the nearest table. She turned it up and looked around her. Now to begin...

Chapter Eight

Life was really quite entertaining when one allowed oneself to pay attention. The charge of the fortune hunters toward Harriet Cole was truly comical. As was her expression of alarm, although for some reason it did not make him laugh. A rumour had sprung up that the girl was an heiress. If she was, what the devil had she been doing on the stagecoach dressed in clothes his sister would not even inflict upon the poor?

Transferring his attention, he was pleased to see James sit by his wife. Astonishing what a swift, verbal kick could accomplish. However, Bab seemed to exist merely to plague him, for a bare ten minutes later she rose and joined a different group. Which was well and good. One had to be sociable, but why in God's name choose the group that contained Illsworth? Was she a complete idiot?

Well she can do her own verbal kicking next time... The thought had barely flitted through his frustrated brain, when he realized Harriet Cole was wading through her flock of admirers and escaping the room. She did not look at Bab. But Bab saw her.

She and Bab had left the dining room together. Bab was convinced Illsworth lied about the cravat pin. Had she recruited another ally?

His breath caught on unexpected laughter. Well, he might be wrong, but it might be amusing to find out. He rose to accept a cup of tea from his amiable hostess. He strolled around to the door with it and abandoned it on the nearest table before leaving the room.

The footmen in the hall bowed to him in unison. One of them closed the door.

Interestingly, a familiar boy and girl were playing on the stairs. His lips twitched as he sauntered in that direction.

"Snake," Orchid greeted him with a surprisingly friendly smile.

"Miss Orchid. Master Alex. What an odd place to play. Shouldn't you be in the nursery?"

"Oh, we're allowed another few minutes," Alex assured him.

"Allowed by your sister, or by the nursemaid?"

"Harriet, of course."

"Of course. Come along, then."

"Along where?" Alex asked, willingly jumping up another few steps.

"To find Harriet, of course."

"She doesn't want to be found," Orchid whispered.

"I know," Sanderly whispered back. "She left you as look-outs."

"Oh, she told you." Alex looked relieved. He waved one hand toward the top of the stairs in a clearly pre-arranged signal. Rose waved back.

"Best keep looking," Sanderly advised. "You would make excellent pickets," he told Rose on the landing.

"What's a picket?"

"A soldier guarding his camp from the enemy."

"Are you going to help Harriet? She's in—"

"I know where she is. Don't tell a soul."

"I wouldn't!" Rose exclaimed, apparently oblivious to the fact that she had been about to blurt it to him.

Sanderly walked on to the left until he came to Illsworth's room. A rather bright light moved and flickered beneath the door. He wondered if the redoubtable Harriet numbered lock-picking among her talents, or if Illsworth just hadn't bothered locking the door. He rather thought the latter, though the former would certainly be more amusing.

Silently, he opened the door and wandered inside. "Good evening, Miss Cole."

She jumped, quite literally, causing the mattress she had been heaving upward to crash back down. As she spun around to face him, her feet must have got tangled in the unruly sheets for she sat down abruptly on the now askew mattress, trying to untangle her trapped feet by kicking and glare at him at the same time.

"Allow me," Sanderly said, advancing.

"I can—"

"Manage?" he suggested, crouching in front of her and loosening the ever-tightening grip of the sheet with ease, now that she was still. "Of course you can, but this is so much simpler. And quicker, more to the point."

When he raised his gaze to her face, she no longer looked panicked.

"So," he said conversationally. "We finally find ourselves alone together in a bedchamber."

To his surprise, she smiled. "I'm sorry it took me so long to realize you were giving us your room. I set off there in high dudgeon, determined to throw your things out and lock you out at the same time."

"An admirable plan. But even I would have balked at amorous advances made under the curious eyes of four children, so you were perfectly safe."

"I was safe because Mrs. George knew you better than I did," she retorted. "She removed your baggage without my instruction."

"Who is Mrs. George?" he asked, deliberately provoking.

"You know perfectly well," she scolded. "I left you a note of thanks, you know, but I think you had gone some time before we did."

About to rise to his feet, he paused, holding her gaze. "Where did you leave this note?"

"In your room, of course, on the mantelshelf. I thought you would reoccupy the room once we had gone."

"What did it say?"

"Just thank you. It was very short."

"I suppose you signed it."

"Of course I did."

Something else to extract from Illsworth, no doubt. "Stand up then and let us see what is beneath this mattress."

He hefted it up and she felt about with both hands.

"Nothing," she said with dissatisfaction.

He let the mattress down again and began to pull the sheets and pillows straight, before tucking everything in.

"I never imagined you were so domesticated."

"Army life is much duller than people imagine. Since you are here, how much of the room have you searched?"

"All of it. He hasn't many things with him and his bags are all empty. Either it really was stolen or he didn't bring it with him after all."

"Or he pawned it."

"Did Lady Bab ask you to help me look?" she asked, kneeling in the middle of the tasteful Persian carpet and feeling it, presumably for cravat-pin shaped lumps.

"Did Lady Bab tell you I had already looked?"

She glanced up. "No, she just said you believed him, and I thought he was a friend of yours, so—"

"What on earth gave you that idea?"

"You were playing dice with him."

He stared at her. "You have a very odd idea of friendship."

At that point, footsteps thundered along the passage along with a breathless childish voice singing a high pitched song in French. Both pattering feet and voice might have belonged to Rose Cole.

"He's coming!" Harriet exclaimed, springing to her feet and grabbing him by the hand. "That's the signal! Quick!"

EVEN AS SHE PULLED Sanderly toward the door, it struck her that one probably should not lug earls around quite so familiarly. However, concentrating on not being caught where she had no business to be—and certainly not with Sanderly—she was only vaguely aware of the startlement in his eyes when she seized his hand. It lay stiffly in her hold, and then abruptly, his fingers curled around hers, halting her at the door while he opened it, peered into the corridor and then he bolted out, tugging her with him.

She had time—just—to close the door behind her and then they were fleeing down the passage hand in hand like a pair of children. His long legs ate up the distance with little apparent effort, while she seemed to fly along and around the bend in the passage that would hide them from anyone approaching from the staircase.

Ahead, the door to the servants' stairs was still swinging, so Rose had clearly made her getaway. An instant's sudden joy surged up, the exhilaration of speed and shared naughtiness mixed with memory of a simpler childhood when life was uncomplicated fun. The vanishing of Sanderly's dignity and the warm clasp of his strong hand had something to do with it too.

But she had only a moment to dwell on it, for the servants' door suddenly swung open again to the sounds of female voices. Maids sent to light lamps or turn down beds or await their mistresses.

Together, Harriet and Sanderly all but skidded to a halt. She tried to yank her hand free to give them at least a faint semblance of respectability. But to her surprise, he held tight and pulled her suddenly to the right before whisking her inside a dark bedchamber.

A key turned unmistakably in the lock.

It came to Harriet that she should probably be afraid, or outraged. Both, probably. And yet she wasn't. The excitement was still with her.

Outside, in the passage, one of the maids laughed. A door opened and closed again. One set of footsteps hurried past. Harriet's heart was still drumming. She could hear Sanderly's breath, quick and uneven, and turned her head toward him. It was too dark to see anything.

"Are you *laughing*?" she whispered.

"Don't be silly," he said unsteadily.

"We can't stay trapped in here."

"No. Sadly not." He released her hand but did not unlock the door.

Her heart jolted. "Is this *your* room?"

"Fortunately not. Imagine the outrage if you were seen emerging from *that* den of iniquity." He moved away from her and that, along with the return to his sardonic manner caused a curious sense of loss.

She heard the striking of flint and a light flared as he lit a candle. By its glow, he looked very tall and thin, almost cadaverous, and yet he was a handsome man when the sneer was not on his lips. And those eyes...she wished she could see them.

Abruptly, her wish was granted. Picking up the candle, he raised his gaze to her face. She could not breathe. Something very odd seemed to be happening to her stomach, her knees. Her mind.

"It is my sister's room. It might be amusing to whip up a scandal for James, but no one would believe it."

"Why don't you like him?"

The straight eyebrows flew up. "Bab likes him. I find that is quite enough."

"You're helping her," Harriet said, making the full discovery for the first time. "That's why you came to Grand Court when you clearly don't care for such parties."

"Only partly." He moved to the door again, listening, before he turned the key in the lock once more. "You should return to the drawing room instantly. I don't trust Illsworth's gift for innuendo."

"You will come a few minutes later?"

"Oh, no, I shall take myself out of the equation altogether and go to bed."

She blinked. "Won't Lady Grandison find you rude?"

"Darling, the world knows I am rude. Don't take all night, there's a good girl."

She turned to face the door, still frowning. "What's your other reason?"

"For what?" he asked, either bewildered or pretending to be.

"For coming to Grand Court."

His lips quirked. He leaned nearer until she could feel his breath—which was good, she assured herself for she didn't appear to have any of her own. "You. Now flee."

He opened the door, looked into the passage and all but pushed her outside. She was hurrying down the servants' stairs before she realized she was not supposed to believe him. He was teasing her, joking because his reasons were really none of her business.

This realization allowed her to breathe again and be comfortable. Only she wasn't entirely. Perhaps because she already knew his other reason was the lovely Mrs. Eldridge, whatever Bab said about their liaison being over.

Emerging miraculously unseen onto the first floor, she quickly found Alex and Orchid at the foot of the stairs.

"Where is Rose?" she asked, very aware of the wooden-faced footmen flanking the drawing room door.

"Gone to see Lily. Did you get her warning?" Alex said anxiously.

"Yes, all is well. You've done excellently, but now you must go to bed. Collect Rose on your way and send for me if Lily is too hot or unwell." She hugged them both at once, and sent them on their way, promising to look in on them in the nursery on her way to bed.

A footman opened the drawing room door for her. But once more her hopes of passing unnoticed were foiled by several gentlemen springing to their feet and surging in her direction.

Feeling rather like a hunted hare, she was relieved by Lady Grandison's summons. "There you are, Harriet. Have you been looking in on poor Lily? How is she?"

As she made her way to her godmother's side, basic courtesy forced her admirers to fall back.

"I left her asleep," Harriet said truthfully. "And have ordered the other children to bed. They seemed to have escaped Mildred." With Harriet's help and encouragement, of course.

"Mischievous little creatures," Lady Grandison said comfortably. "You are quite the mother to them. Sadly you have missed our musical entertainment. Miss Leslie and Miss Williams have been playing and singing for us most delightfully."

"I'm sorry to have missed it. I do enjoy music."

"I would love to hear you play, Miss Cole," said Mr. Poole.

Harriet laughed. "No, you would not, sir. I cannot play at all."

"Were you never taught?" Mrs. Eldridge asked. It was the first thing the woman had said to her.

"Oh, I had teachers, but my silly brain would not make the connections between the notes on the page and the keys on the piano."

Several ladies smiled with pity, false or otherwise. Harriet hoped her lack of ladylike accomplishments might deter her sudden wave of admirers, but Lady Grandison would not allow it.

"But you do sing charmingly," she said. "I recall that your voice is quite beautiful."

"If she sings the right notes," Mrs. Eldridge said smiling. "We must not pester the poor lady."

It was the "poor lady" that did it.

"Well, if you play for me, ma'am, I shall do my poor best."

She sang a happy song with a dancing rhythm that she was glad to see both brightened the company and restored her and therefore her godmother to the ranks of the accomplished and un-pitied. At least partially.

While she was singing, Illsworth re-entered the room. She hoped they had left his bedchamber exactly as he had.

After one song and her gracious acceptance of the surprised applause, Bab seized on her and she was able to report. "Nothing."

"Really? Then Snake was right, drat the man."

"I looked everywhere I could think of."

Bab's breath caught. "What if he carries it with him?"

Harriet gazed at her. "Well I am not creeping up on him while he's asleep."

Bab giggled.

※

IN THE MORNING, LILY felt so much better that she wanted to get up. Harriet forbade it.

"It's still very early, and you were so weak yesterday. Let us wait until after breakfast, which you must have in bed—though the children and I will keep you company if you wish. After that, we shall see."

Lily smiled at her, half-mocking, wholly affectionate, and much more like herself. "Where would we be without you, Mama Harry?"

Harriet laughed, although the words brought a serious worry to the fore. What *would* they do without her at school? Could she rely on anyone to look after the children if and when they were ill? Rose was only ten years old and could not be expected to care for the more delicate Lily if and when she was sick. Orchid was little more than a baby. And Alex would be without any of them.

As she washed and donned the walking dress that had miraculously appeared in her wardrobe along with another afternoon gown, she thought rather hard about her original plan to become a governess. Leaving Lily with a novel to read, she first checked that the children were still asleep in the nursery—they were—and then escaped the house for a brisk walk before breakfast. Fresh air always helped her to think.

When she took up the post as governess, she could not take the children with her.

And another difficulty had struck her yesterday evening. Who would employ a governess who could not teach her charges to read music or play the pianoforte?

Drat and damnation!

On the other hand... Her breath caught on yet another idea. "That is it!"

The trees to her left rustled with more than the wind, startling her and she whipped around to see a man halted a bare yard away on a very faint, narrow path which led off the main one.

"*What* is it?" Lord Sanderly inquired.

Chapter Nine

It was more than relief that caused her involuntary smile. She was pleased to see him. "I'm still thinking about it," she replied to his question. "Good morning, my lord."

"Good morning, Miss Cole. We must stop meeting like this."

"Don't be silly. I have never met you in a wood before."

"Well be sure you never do so again."

"You know, I never expected you to be quite so self-deprecating."

"I'm not," he said in apparent surprise. "I'm warning you of the dangers of solitary walks."

"I was brought up in the country," she said scornfully.

"Well, don't let me keep you."

"Are you going back for breakfast?"

"They don't even begin breakfast until eleven."

"Well, you may walk with me if you like and tell me what you think of my new idea."

For an instant, he hesitated, and she realized she must seem horribly forward.

"Although you wouldn't possibly be interested," she added hastily. "I shall leave you to your own walk."

"No, don't," he said, falling into step beside her. "What are you up to now?"

"Well, originally I thought I would be a governess while the children went away to school."

"Why do you want to be a governess?"

"To feed myself and pay the school fees."

A frown flickered on his brow.

"From my salary," she said by way of explanation.

"My dear girl, how far do you imagine a governess's pay stretches?"

"Well, I don't precisely know. Is it not enough?" She felt curiously deflated.

"No," he said flatly.

"Oh well, it doesn't really matter, for I have thought of a better plan. I could not take the children with me if I was a governess, but if I taught at a school instead, then perhaps the children could stay and be educated at that school. It still leaves Alex alone, of course, but I'm sure I'll come up with something. What do you think?"

He was looking at her rather oddly. "I think you should get your family's lawyers to force your cousin Randolph to pay. I am presuming your fortune is left in trust for you."

She frowned. How did he know about Randolph? The children, or even Lady Grandison, must have been talking to him. She might have felt ashamed, except his manner was so accepting of the situation and he was clearly on her side.

"I never heard of any lawyers," she said honestly. "Randolph has everything."

"But you must be housed and educated."

She wrinkled her nose. "We don't like being housed by Randolph. I'm convinced the winter cold and the hard work has made Lily ill. We have to look after ourselves." She frowned. "But you know, Lady Bab made the same mistake as you. She seems to think we are much richer than we are. Oh!"

He paused when she did, his hand holding back a tree branch from her path. "What enlightenment have you received?"

"All those young men," she said, trying not to laugh. "*That* is why they were suddenly so attentive! They think I'm an heiress too... Well that is a relief."

"You are pleased to be the object of fortune hunters?"

"Oh no, it's just I was afraid they had recognized me from the Duck and Spoon and were playing some kind of trick." She walked past him.

Letting the branch go, he strode along beside her. He drew in a breath. "I suppose this is really where I should apologize for kissing you."

It was so unexpected, she could not prevent the heat burning up to her ears. At least she managed to mutter. "Don't worry. It doesn't matter. I know you didn't mean it. I expect you were foxed."

"Oh, I was," he said, and in spite of everything, disappointment crept into her heart. "I would otherwise have been more circumspect. Sobriety might have stopped me kissing you, though it wouldn't have stopped me wanting to."

"It wouldn't?" Her whole face seemed to be on fire. "I might be flattered, only I expect one woman is much like another to men in their cups egging each other on."

A breath of laughter escaped him. "Do you never accept a compliment?"

"I'm not perfectly sure I received one. And in any case, neither do you."

"Oh, I *never* receive any."

"Then I will tell you, you are a kind and honourable man."

"I am not," he said, as though revolted.

She laughed. "Then why are you helping Bab? Why did you give us your room at the inn? Along with the means to keep everyone else out?"

The heavy eyelids lifted, revealing his startling, beautiful eyes. For an instant, neither of them seemed to breathe. "I forget."

"No you don't. Why do you pretend to be unpleasant?"

"My dear child, I *am* unpleasant."

"No you're not, though you seem to work quite hard at appearing so. And neither am I a child."

"True," he agreed. "Does that mean I can kiss you again?"

"No," she said, frowning. "Not like that."

"Like what then?" he mocked.

"You have to mean it," she blurted.

He stared at her. "Mean what? What do you think I meant the last time?"

"I think you meant to show the others you could immediately do what they were working up to, thereby annoying them and proving your own reputation at the same time."

His lips curled and he moved on. "There, you see. I *am* unpleasant."

His voice was mockingly victorious and yet there was some bitter truth there, too. She wanted to take his hand, hug him. But he was not a little boy to be so easily soothed.

What happened to you? At least she did not say that aloud, for she was sure he would merely walk away and never speak to her again.

"You can't be," she said mildly. "The children like you. If they didn't, they would have warned me last night before you got anywhere near Illsworth's room."

"I hate to imagine what song that would have necessitated."

Harriet laughed but felt obliged to defend her little sister. "It's hard to sing while pelting along a corridor at full tilt."

"I shall test the theory some time when I am alone and very, very bored."

"If you expect to be bored abroad, why are you going?"

"I am preparing for all eventualities. My goal is obviously *not* to be bored."

"You are escaping from boredom?" she said carefully.

"Present company excepted."

"There is no need to be polite on my account."

His lips twisted. "Curiously enough, I am not."

THE THOUGHT WAS SOMETHING of a blinding revelation to Sanderly. Not just that she didn't bore him—that, after all, was insultingly faint praise—but he enjoyed her company. If he hadn't, he would have walked on this morning without letting himself be seen. He would not have sought her out last night when he suspected her of doing Bab's dirty work. Hell and the devil confound it, he probably wouldn't have come to Grand Court at all if he hadn't known she would be here.

A twinge of guilt twisted through him. He owed Bab more than that. He would have sailed without even saying goodbye, leaving her to face her marital crisis alone. Oh, he had made sure she would always be taken care of financially, that all the family homes were at her disposal whenever she wanted or needed them. But that was not being her brother.

How far had he fallen in his petulance against society? Bab had never shunned him, never deserved to be ignored, even for marrying against his advice. For some reason, it had taken this girl, a complete stranger, to make that clear to him. He had become in reality what he had pretended to be in his defensive, all-consuming jest.

And yet there had to be something of himself left. This girl didn't give two hoots for his reputation. Nor for his title or riches, or sensual pleasures—although he was only too aware of the desire to introduce her to the latter. He amused her. She treated him as a friend when he had done nothing to deserve that honour.

Even now, she was chattering on, asking him questions about his journey. With difficulty, he dredged up some off-hand answer, but she only persevered, and he found himself talking about the wonders he had glimpsed in his military travels, and his promise to himself to go back to explore one day, about all he had learned in reading and talking to people who had explored further south than the north African coast.

Her wide eyes sparkled with interest. She asked questions and drank in his answers as though his enthusiasm was infectious.

And that was when the insidious thought hit him. That his journey would be more fun with her. That his life...

Woah! Genuinely terrified, he whipped around suddenly, increasing his pace to escape her suddenly intolerable company.

"Is it breakfast time?" she asked in amusement.

"If it isn't, it should be."

"I had better make sure the children are in order and that Lily doesn't get up while my back is turned."

"Do you never do anything for yourself?" he asked, unreasonably irritated. "Does your whole life revolve around those children?"

"Yes, I suppose it does," she said cheerfully.

Which explained her fascination with *his* conversation. "Then your chances of doing anything remotely to your taste are negligible."

She did not wilt, or quarrel. She only cast him a quick, clear look, a faint frown tugging at her pretty brow. "Why are you angry?"

"I am never angry," he drawled.

"Yes, you are. I think it is all anger."

Intolerable. Humiliating. Impossible. "Deluded child..." Relief was in sight. They were almost out of the woods and he could send her away with the excuse of her reputation. And never speak to her again. Which meant there were things he had to say now.

"Involve Grandison and the lawyers in your inheritance. Something is very wrong about your cousin's behaviour. And avoid Illsworth like the plague. Never be alone with him or give him any advantage. Now run along before anyone suspects I have ruined you."

He strode away from her, heading back into the wood in the vague direction of the stables, carrying with him his last sight of her wide eyes, surprised and hurt and...

Who the devil cares? he asked himself savagely. *I don't. The sooner I get away from here the better.*

An hour later, he was throwing his clothes into bags when a peremptory knock heralded the invasion of his sister.

"Oh, Snake, the most..." She broke off, taking in the scene before her. "What are you doing?"

"Packing."

"But—but where are you going?"

"Harwich," he said patiently. "In the first instance."

"But...but you don't even know now when the next ship will sail where you want to go, let alone whether you may book passage on it. I thought you had given up the idea."

"I postponed it—at considerable inconvenience and cost, I might add—in order to do what you asked of me. Having done so, I feel entitled to the reward of departure."

"But James is still cool, because I laughed with Cedric yesterday evening, and I still don't have my pin!"

"Tell James. He clearly does not want to lose your affections, so you might as well be honest. It's only a cravat pin."

"It is a *love* token! Or at least it was. Why was I such a fool?"

"Look, Illsworth doesn't have it. Whether stolen or pawned, it's not coming back to haunt you. Things get lost all the time."

"Yes, but it might. Harriet and I worked out that he could have had the pin about his person while—" She broke off, eyeing Sanderly with a touch of guilt.

"While she searched his room. If it hadn't been for her family lookouts, he would have caught her there."

"Oh, don't, Snake. I feel so horrible about it already. I just could not keep him there any longer, short of hanging onto his arm and that would hardly have gone down well with James!"

"Or me," Sanderly said austerely. "The point is—"

"Oh, I know what the point is," she interrupted. "You needn't lecture me in that odiously self-righteous manner when Alicia Eldridge practically sits on your lap in public."

"Shocking, is it not? Some women just court notoriety. Stay away from Illsworth."

"Stay away from Mrs. Eldridge," Bab retorted. "She's poisonous." She laughed. "From a snake-bite no doubt."

"Leave it, Bab," he said irritably. "I needed a reason to be here when I had already declined, and that reason should not be the marital idiocy of my sister."

Bab's jaw dropped. "Oh, Snake." She sat down on the bed. "Only it's not very kind to Mrs. Eldridge, is it?"

He shrugged. "She understands the game better than most. And if it makes you feel better, I haven't laid a finger on her for months. Nor do I intend to."

"You should tell her, not me."

"I did. I daresay her wrath will become another reason for my fleeing the country."

"Then don't go. Don't let them drive you out of your own seat, your own country."

Sanderly dropped his hairbrushes into the top of the bag. "My dear Bab, wherever did you get the notion that anyone at all influences what I choose to do?"

"God knows," she said bitterly, springing to her feet once more. "Must have been from the sweet little boy you used to be. Goodbye, Snake. Enjoy your journey."

"Enjoy yours," he said to her retreating back.

The door slammed, which gave him no satisfaction. After all, he had just alienated the last member of his family who tolerated him. His last sibling. His last tie with his parents and Hugo and their shared past.

Without warning, he swung up his right foot and kicked his bag off the bed. It flew across the room, emptying its contents with a clatter and landed upside down beneath the window.

※

BREAKFASTING IN HER bedchamber with the children, Harriet was impressed to see them in clothes that not only almost fitted them but looked good as new. Admittedly, they were a trifle old-fashioned, but the children didn't care for that. On the contrary, even Alex seemed rather proud.

"How smart you look!" Harriet exclaimed.

"Her ladyship kept things from every stage of her own children's growing up," said Mildred, who had escorted them to the room to learn Harriet's wishes. "It's good to see them being used."

Harriet hoped her godmother would not miss them. "I expect we'll go out for the morning," she told the maid.

"Me too," Lily said eagerly.

"We'll try you out first," Harriet said, which turned out to be a good if worrying decision. For Lily, having walked three times around the bedchamber in her dressing gown, sank back onto the bed with tears in her eyes.

"Oh, don't worry, Lil, it will take time," Harriet said, putting her arm around her. "Have a good rest this morning, and then perhaps in the afternoon you will be up to getting dressed and sitting in the garden." Only, it was a long way to the garden…

"I could give you a piggyback," Alex said cheerfully, which at least led to insults and banter while Harriet urged Lily back into bed, where she soon fell asleep.

She accompanied the other children outside to the grounds, where they played hide and seek in the maze and then tried pall-mall on the lawn. It was here that Lady Grandison found them, beaming to see them in such high spirits.

"Lily is still very tired," Harriet told her.

"I'll send for Dr. Bagshott. I daresay he has a tonic of some kind that will help. But it seems to me you have all been shabbily treated by Randolph Cole. To call it no worse."

"Do you know who my parents' solicitor is?"

Lady Grandison blinked. "No, but Sir John might. We'll speak to him later. Now, my dear, about your plans to become a governess.…"

Harriet sighed. "They won't work, will they? Even if anyone would employ me, I would not earn nearly enough to send any of them to school."

"I don't believe you would," Lady Grandison said, with rather obvious relief.

"I was thinking a better plan would be to teach in a school. They might not care there that I cannot read music properly—I daresay they will have enough teachers who can. And I expect I could keep the girls with me, even if it used up all my salary. Which still leaves Alex. Would it be awful of me to ask Sir John for a loan to send Alex to school? It would not need to be Eton or Harrow, and I could easily pay him back as soon as I am five-and-twenty."

"That is one plan, and I daresay Sir John would go along with it," Lady Grandison said cautiously. "But perhaps you should not rush into anything just yet? Consider that you might wish to be married instead."

"I don't," Harriet said in surprise.

"Whyever not?"

"Well, consider being married to Cousin Randolph, for example. There would be no escape then!"

"No, but you need not marry Randolph. In fact, I would counsel strongly against it! You are a very charming and beautiful girl. Any number of men will wish to marry you, so you might, you know, take your pick. Then you may be happy as well as financially comfortable, and your husband will keep Randolph in line."

Harriet gazed at her with some respect. "You have thought it all out."

"Well, I could not quite like the idea of you going for a governess, not even for a few years. I feel this is a much more comfortable plan. There are many eligible gentlemen at Grand Court just now, and then there are several other parties elsewhere before the spring when I can give you a proper Season. Which is always what your dear mother and I planned."

"But that would mean months of us living off you! And you know, ma'am, I find I do not like to be...dependent."

Lady Grandison sighed and took her arm. "It is a fact of life, my dear, that females are always dependent on men to some degree. Particularly females of our station in life. At least this way, you get to choose which man to be dependent upon, and that is no small thing, believe me. You see how it worked out for you parents, and for Sir John and me. And there need be no worry about the children or a home for them with you until they fly the nest."

"That is true. But I cannot think anyone would want me as a wife. I am far too managing and outspoken and—"

"Don't be silly, child. I could name five men who are already courting you."

Harriet laughed. "Only because they somehow acquired the idea that I am wealthy!"

Lady Grandison blushed. "You are not poor. I merely exaggerated a trifle, just to obtain you a little attention to start you off. I don't mean you should necessarily marry Dolt or Fool, I mean Poole, although they are actually well bred enough. I would not have Wriggley, though. But they have served their purpose. More serious men have noticed your popularity and therefore you. Sir Ralph and Mr. Thornton, for example. I'm sure even Sanderly was watching you in the drawing room before he vanished."

"Was he?" Harriet was surprised but did not like the wistfulness in her own voice.

"Not that I would wish him on you," her godmother said hastily. "Not quite the thing for all he's an earl. But—"

"What does society have against Lord Sanderly?" she asked bluntly. "Lots of gentlemen are rakes or just rude. Why do they pick on him?"

"Oh, it all started with him being cashiered from the army. No one really knows why —or, actually, *whether* he was cashiered or resigned. But either way, it was dishonourably. Either he was a cheat, or a traitor, or struck a general, or all three. Anyway, he came home in disgrace to take up his late brother's place as earl. He pays little attention to the ton, making very erratic appearances to bankrupt the foolish at dice or flaunt lovers in front of their husband's noses."

"Why do men play him if he cheats? Why does he have lovers if he is so awful? Why did you invite him?"

Lady Grandison began to look a little flustered, patting her hair and walking a little faster. "One must respect the title, and the old earl… I didn't think he'd accept, and he didn't. Only then he changed his mind. But you must see it brings a little cachet if someone refuses every other hostess and then attends *my* party."

"Even if he cheats and rakes his way around it?"

"My dear," Lady Grandison said in shocked tones. "I don't believe he has. Besides, he still means to flee the country. My maid said he was packing."

"Today?" Harriet's dismay was quite out of proportion to her acquaintance with Sanderly. And she had not hidden it. Her godmother's shrewd gaze lingered on her face with mingled alarm and pity.

"You must not even look in that quarter. I agree he can be charming when he chooses, and he can certainly reduce the room to tears of laughter—though I did prefer his humour before it grew quite so barbed…"

"I am not looking in any quarter," Harriet said hastily. "I just feel a lot of people who criticize him are like pots calling the kettle black. None of it is my concern. I like Sir Ralph, though his eyes are terribly sad. What is his story?"

"Crossed in love, I believe," Lady Grandison said, "or so his mother once told me. But he is not at all melancholic in his manner and you could do a great deal worse…"

Harriet let her chatter, glad to have distracted her. In fact, she had no intention of marrying anyone…although perhaps she really should consider it? Her godmother was right that marriage would open the way to her own money and provide a home and security for the children. Those were no small things. Was it selfish of her to long for independence and freedom?

At any rate, she rather thought she had been naïve about the freedoms of a poorly paid governess, and it was quite possible that a school teacher would have less yet. No wonder people married for money and convenience.

Could I? She let a line of all the single gentlemen she had ever met drift through her mind. When she tried to imagine them sitting by the fireside with her, walking with her, even dancing with her, she could not do it.

And then, without warning, she remembered Sanderly's insolent kiss. And before she could avoid it, she envisioned him lying beside her in bed, his blue eyes blazing as he took her into his arms, and her whole being melted in a torrent of half-understood desires.

Oh dear God, what does this mean?

Chapter Ten

He didn't go, Harriet thought with ridiculously out-of-proportion relief as she entered the garden room and saw Lord Sanderly filling his plate with delicacies from the luncheon table.

"He didn't go," Bab exclaimed beside her. "Or at least, not yet."

"You think he still might?" Harriet murmured.

"Well, he was packed and ready before eleven o'clock this morning, and my temper caused me to scold him rather than persuade him to stay. It was almost a relief to find he still has one too."

"Has one what?" Harriet asked, bewildered.

"Temper. Are you looking forward to the afternoon's treasure hunt? We are all to have partners, I believe, decided by Lady G. Which means I shan't have my James."

James, in fact, was seated with Mrs. Eldridge near the garden door. Sanderly strolled past them with his plate, appeared to notice them for the first time, and laughed. Which sparked a quite inappropriate mirth in Harriet.

"They're probably trying to make you both jealous," she whispered hastily to Bab.

"Well it's working for me," Bab said bleakly. "Snake says I should tell James the truth. What do you think?"

"It might be better than all this doubt."

"What if it's worse?"

Bab was not, Harriet reflected, the best of models to tempt her to marriage. Bab was miserable and so was James, and they began, apparently, as a love match. What chance of happiness did other couples stand?

"There are two vacant chairs at their table," Harriet pointed out.

"I should be mortified," Bab said, appalled.

"I rather think it is she who will be mortified."

In fact, although she recovered quickly, Mrs. Eldridge did look momentarily disconcerted. And Bab played her part to perfection, making pleasant conversation with the utmost friendliness, as if she and her husband had decided together who they would sit with.

Harriet began to wish for the uncomplicated company of the children. Or at least some of Sanderly's humour. Perhaps she would be paired with him for the treasure hunt...

She wasn't, of course. Her godmother, aware of her liking, had given her Sir Ralph as her partner.

"We could probably win this," Harriet said cheerfully, when they had found their third clue. "I wonder what the treasure is?"

"What would you like it to be?"

A couple came out of the orchard, crossing their path. The lady all but danced with excitement. The gentleman, who looked only too familiar, pointed toward the wood, and strolled on, apparently deaf to her clear urging to greater speed.

Harriet's heart gave an odd little lurch. She cast a quick, surreptitious glance at Sir Ralph to be sure she had betrayed nothing and found him gazing still at the same couple. His expression was unreadable.

"You don't like him," Harriet said, guessing her companion had recognized Sanderly too.

"No one likes him. Or admits to it."

"Why is that?"

"Fashion. The lake is this way."

"Are earls not always fashionable?" She fell into step beside him.

Sir Ralph did not answer for several moments. "He is his own worst enemy. He was very popular at school. He arrived at Eton during my final year there and thrived almost immediately. Not just because Hugo looked out for him, either."

"Who is Hugo?"

"The late earl, Snake's older brother. Snake went into the army. Thrived there, too. Mentioned in dispatches."

Was that a note of pride in his voice? "Is he your friend?" she blurted.

Sir Ralph's smile was twisted. He shook his head. "No. We were never friends. But everyone was glad to follow his career in those days. Then it all changed."

"When?"

"About eighteen months ago, when Sanderly—Hugo—died. Snake came home as the new earl, but under a cloud. Rumours flew that he had been cashiered, though whether for cheating at cards, for striking a fellow officer, or for treachery was hotly debated. Others declared he had resigned his commission to avoid being cashiered. His old commanding officers never defended him. His family turned against him. Hugo's betrothed gave him a very public cut direct. He isn't invited to many places. If he is, he doesn't usually go. Several clubs have blackballed him. But there he is. Or at least, he's in there somewhere. Maybe."

"You care," she said, frowning.

His eyes fell and he shrugged. "I am a student of human nature. I suspect you are, too."

Harriet took his arm, an acknowledgement of their shared fascination. It was almost like a conspiracy as well as a new, warming friendship. And the ache of human tragedies. "There is the lake," she said brightly. "What exactly did the clue say?"

<hr />

ILLSWORTH WAS DELIGHTED that Lady Grandison had heeded his discreet request to be partnered with Bab Fforbes. He barely even thought of her by her husband's name for the man was a nonentity. The fool, attending a dull debutante, did not even seem to notice as his wife went blithely off on Illsworth's arm.

Neither did Sanderly, although somehow Illsworth doubted he was unaware of it. He had not expected Snake to intervene at all, so his visit last night to demand the return of Bab's gift had taken him by surprise. Naturally this would not prevent Illsworth from pursuing the liaison. It even added an extra little thrill of danger. Not much, though, for although one remembered his youthful temper, his blows these days were merely verbal. Even Snake would not insult his own sister in public. And in any case, he would soon be gone from these shores.

Somewhere, Illsworth knew this was too comfortable an assessment. Unconsciously, he was touching his cravat, recalling the surprising strength of the fingers twisting the fabric until he genuinely feared being strangled. But of course it had not happened. Snake would never risk his own neck. Though he was a damned good actor.

But Bab was always amusing company, even though Illsworth's favourite thing was merely to look at her, appreciating her beauty and the luscious, tempting curves he would soon caress and kiss and bend to his sensual will. The fact that she paid no attention to his secret touches and devoted if lustful looks, only encouraged his ardour.

Of course, following the clues—largely to Bab's understanding since Illsworth's focus was elsewhere—held a certain frustration, for there was nowhere in the grounds one was not liable to come across another couple or three. Just as he was about to take Bab in his arms, they would fall over people ferreting under hedges or garden seats, dipping hands—and sleeves—in the lake in search of clues. Inevitably Bab would make conversation with them while Illsworth, smiling amiably, wished them all to the devil.

Still, he made some use of the time for his other plans.

"You seem quite friendly with Lady Grandison's goddaughter," he remarked.

"Miss Cole? Yes, I like her. So unaffected and refreshing. She makes me laugh."

"I'm sorry that is such a rarity in your life."

Bab laughed, no doubt to disprove his words.

"Is she truly a great heiress, then?" he asked idly.

Bab cast him a quick glance that was not entirely friendly. "So I believe, though she sets no store by it if she is."

Excellent. Bab was jealous. "A privilege of the extremely wealthy. Why has she had no Season then?"

Bab shrugged. "Mourning, I suppose. Her father died recently, I believe, so he was probably ill before that."

"Ah. So there is nothing wrong with her birth, or her family?"

"Don't be silly, Cedric. Do you take Lady Grandison for a fool?"

"I take her to be soft-hearted," Illsworth said dryly. "Sir John, on the other hand, is fairly shrewd."

"So you plan to join the throngs of other fortune hunters already snapping around the poor girl?"

"No, my dear, I plan to stand out from among said fortune hunters."

"Well, if you hurt my friend, I shall be forced to cut you."

"Never do that, Bab," he said seriously, and she laughed.

"This is the third gate...Yes, there is a note nailed to it!"

There were also voices coming from the maze beyond. Illsworth sighed and bided his time.

Finally, when frustration was beginning to seriously wear down his temper, they came to the oak at the edge of the wood. Bab walked around it until it shielded her from most of the grounds. For once, no one else lurked nearby.

As Bab reached up to the branch and the note tied there with string, Illsworth pounced, closing his arms around her from behind.

"Bab, my divine angel. You truly are irresistible." Since she jumped rather alarmingly at his touch, he tightened his grip, but to his delight, she showed no desire to flee. And God, she was a delectable armful, soft and scented. "One kiss," he said huskily.

"Not from this angle," she said, laughing, although she turned in his arms and brought one hand up to his cheek. He tried to kiss it, but somehow her fingers stayed in place with surprising firmness. He bent his head to claim her lips, but her grip had moved, holding his chin.

"Don't be naughty, Cedric."

"No one can see."

"Not the point. You must not ruin a perfectly amusing friendship, you know."

"I can be a much more amusing lover," he said ardently, then wished he hadn't, for it made her giggle instead of melt. He pushed against her grip of his chin, and since he was by far the stronger, he would have succeeded in his pursuit of her luscious lips—only quite suddenly he realized her hand was in his coat pocket.

At first, lust surged through him at such intimacy, such eagerness, until it came to him what she was about.

She was still looking for the damned cravat pin.

She must have seen the knowledge in his eyes, for her hand slipped out of his pocket and they stared at each other. Which was precisely the moment Martindale stepped out of the nearest thicket.

"Oh damn and blast you, Cedric," Bab whispered, whisking herself out of his hold.

Illsworth began to laugh, mostly because Martindale was not doing the sensible thing of pretending not to see. He even ignored his partner, the plain debutante, to stride purposefully toward them with a face like thunder.

Bab strode away, clearly expecting Illsworth to follow and avoid the inevitable scene. He couldn't make up his mind whether to do so and maintain his pursuit or give in to the mischievous part of his nature and rile Martindale. This was, after all, why he had refused to give back the pin and had truly meant to wear it in front of Bab's husband.

On the other hand, Martindale did look unexpectedly furious with his blazing eyes and twisted mouth; and causing too much of a rumpus at the Grandisons' party would be considered bad form. Illsworth made his decision and had just started after Bab when she all but ran into Sanderly, approaching from the right with Mrs. Ralston.

Although Snake did not look remotely angry, Illsworth knew that this arrival on the scene was much more dangerous. He had to remind himself that Sanderly was a coward and fought only with his tongue. And cravats twisted around his windpipe...

Bab should, of course, have walked straight past her brother before he could notice there was anything amiss, but either she still harboured some childness fondness for the man or he had some hold over her, for she stopped dead in her tracks and Illsworth could hardly walk on without her.

Snake's hooded eyes flickered, but that was the only sign he gave of being remotely interested in the approaching drama.

"Bab in a hurry," he remarked. "Which can only mean one thing. You are about to discover the treasure."

"I am," she said a little wildly. "So let me pass this instant."

"I shouldn't worry, you are clearly miles ahead and James seems to want a word."

Bab's eyes clearly spat *Imbecile!* at him. Or perhaps, *Traitor*!

Amused, Illsworth turned to face the storming Martindale, who was almost unrecognizable in his anger—or was it simple jealousy?

"Ah, Martindale," he said, as though surprised. "How fares your treasure hunt?"

Unexpectedly, Sanderly inserted himself between them, just as Illsworth saw Martindale's fists had clenched purposefully.

"Dear me," Snake drawled. "A gentlemen's confabulation is clearly in order. Perhaps the ladies would oblige us with a moment before Bab and Illsworth make their final charge and capture the treasure. There is a charming bench mere yards beyond you."

Illsworth did not object. He was more entertained than anything else. Bab's gaze flew from her brother to her husband, who was still ignoring her, though now in favour of Sanderly.

Her breath caught. "Come, ladies, let our partners confer while we enjoy a more comfortable rest upon the shady bench. I must admit my feet hurt..." She had enough force of character to sweep off the plain debutante and Mrs. Ralston.

As soon as they were out of earshot, Martindale spoke between his teeth. "I will not have your filthy hands upon my wife. Name—"

"Tut, tut, don't be hasty," Sanderly interrupted, at his most annoyingly urbane. "Ignore Illsworth's filthy hands for one moment and consider that if you duel, the world will know exactly what—and who—is the cause of your quarrel."

"I don't mind," Illsworth drawled. "If Martindale does not."

"No, you probably don't," Sanderly agreed, lifting his eyelids just enough to reveal the unexpected steel in his blue eyes. "But then, you have always been something of a commoner."

Illsworth straightened, startled. "Now, look here—"

"Bad form to paw any unwilling woman," Snake said, sounding more bored than angry. But it was all studied insolence. "Even worse ton to do so in front of company and the lady's husband. If it wasn't for the lady's fair name, I would quite happily walk away and leave James to beat you to a pulp."

Illsworth laughed angrily. "If he thinks he could, he may try!"

"He may not," Sanderly said softly. His gaze was not even on Illsworth, but on Martindale. "As he now understands the damage it would do to his wife. Challenge me, you execrable pile of abject cowardice."

Illsworth laughed, thinking for an instant that Snake had lost his mind and meant to fight Martindale, who most certainly presented less of a threat. Then he saw the blue gaze had shifted once more to him.

Illsworth's jaw dropped, even as furious heat surged through him at such insults.

Martindale said angrily, "You will not fight my battles for me, Sanderly!"

"I'm fighting my own and they take precedence over your quarrel. Well, going to run away rather than face me, Illsworth? That will make a fine tale to spread."

"Stop it, Sanderly," Martindale commanded, frowning in bewilderment. "I will fight him."

"Wrong, but don't feel too badly. You may be my second."

"You're serious," Illsworth said, staring at him. "I think your brains are addled."

"Does he fear the madman?" Sanderly asked Martindale. "Or will he decide it makes me easier to beat?"

Illsworth had had enough. "Damn you, I do call you out! Wolf will be my second."

Sanderly sighed. "Be your age, Illsworth. We must keep the matter between us, which means you must choose someone with a motive to be discreet. Someone like...Sir John Grandison, perhaps."

Martindale spoke, staring at his brother-in-law as though he had grown horns. "You want to involve Grandison? At his own party? What were you saying about bad ton?"

"What was I saying about discretion?"

It was clever, Illsworth admitted reluctantly. It was such bad form, Illsworth would never admit having done it. None of them would. If Illsworth went along with it. And quite suddenly, he thought he would. Sanderly was a thorn in his side where Bab was concerned, and he had seen the heiress Miss Cole watching him too. He should try not to kill Sanderly, of course, but having him out of the way while he recovered would most certainly work in Illsworth's favour.

"Have everything your own way, dear boy. Tomorrow at dawn?"

Sanderly considered. "Too quick. We must give our seconds time to reconcile us."

For the first time since he had known him, Martindale laughed.

Sanderly's lip twitched, but he otherwise paid no attention. "Will you speak to Grandison? Or must I do that for you, too? Come, gentlemen, we must not keep the ladies waiting, and Bab is desperate to win the prize."

"Oh she is," Illsworth said softly, presenting his back to the incandescent husband.

"If only he knew," Sanderly said in a voice of entirely false affection, "what the prize was."

SEEING AT ONCE THAT they were too late to win the treasure hunt, Sanderly apologised to his partner, whom he abandoned at the first available opportunity, and strode off toward the house to think.

He knew exactly what Bab had been doing with Illsworth and her folly appalled him. Quite apart from the ruin of her marriage, she risked considerable physical danger from an entitled man like Illsworth whose only motives were mischief and money.

Sanderly had been forced to step in to prevent James from creating a huge scandal out of an indiscreet instant, but he rather looked forward to hurting Illsworth. No one would think twice about Snake Sanderly committing the solecism of a duel at his hostess's party, and there could be any number of insulting reasons for it. James could only ever have had one reason—Bab—and the world would have known it.

Illsworth quite definitely had to be stopped in his tracks before Sanderly could shake the dust of England from his boots. Perhaps he should just kill him. After all, he was fleeing the country anyway. Though a murder charge might make it awkward to return, even for a peer of the realm...

No, he probably shouldn't kill him.

Walking off his annoyance, he had already passed the garden door and the front door. He kept walking until he came across a small child sitting on the step from another side door onto a small terrace where a round table and several chairs had been set up. The child was crying.

"I want Lily if I can't have Harry," Orchid Cole wailed. "It's not fair. Why can't we have tea all together just for once?"

"Well it's much better than at home," Alex said bracingly from inside the house. "Where we barely got tea at all, let alone a slap up feast like this one."

"Lily will come next time," Rose said, sitting down on the step beside her. "And probably Harry too. But we knew she'd have to spend time with the grown-ups."

"I want Lily *now*. Oh, Snake!" Orchid burst into fresh tears at the sight of him. "Can't you fetch Lily for us? The footmen are all too busy with the adult tea on the big terrace."

"I hesitate to suggest it," Sanderly said, sauntering up to them, just glad that the child had temporarily stopped howling, "but why don't *you* fetch her down?"

"It's too far for her," Rose said. "All those stairs and great long passages. She can only manage three times around the bedroom and then she wilts, and Harriet will be furious if we make her iller. Besides, we don't want to."

"No, I can see that," Sanderly said gravely. "Should she be outside?"

"The doctor—and Harriet!—both said she could be if someone carried her down and she did not get cold. Only there's no one to carry her down. She says she's too big for Alex to carry on his back, and she might be, even though she's so thin—"

"She's not a giant, is she?" Sanderly asked.

They all laughed, even Orchid whose tears had magically disappeared.

"Well in that case, take me to her. I shall wait in the passage while you tell her the plan and make sure she has warm shawls. And if she wishes to join you, she shall."

They all cheered at this. Orchid climbed up onto the waiting chair, and Alex told her to stop bouncing. Chattering constantly, Rose led him into the house and up the staircase to the family's quarters. It did seem to be a very long way.

Rose burst into a bedchamber without knocking and Sanderly realized with inexplicable shock that this was Harriet's bedroom as well as Lily's.

A pale, thin girl of about fourteen summers drooped in an armchair. She was fully dressed with a shawl around her shoulders.

"Guess what, Lil?" Rose cried. "You're coming to tea after all! I've brought Lord Snake, I mean Sanderly, to carry you down! Isn't that wonderful?"

The girl brightened so suddenly that it was like an instant reward. He must be going soft.

Lily rose to her feet. Rose snatched up an extra shawl and a folded blanket from the foot of one bed, while Sanderly found his attention rivetted on the other. This was where Harriet slept, where she was alone with her thoughts and dreams and worries...and her sick sister.

Still, what did she dream of? What did such an unfailing if naïve optimist want from the world? Or did she think only of what she could give? Who she could make better, make happy? Did she ever think of marriage, as girls were supposed to, of love and intimacy...?

Throwing a stern, silent word at himself, Sanderly said amiably, "I shan't drop you, so don't look so worried. May I?"

She smiled rather shyly and nodded, so he lifted her around the waist and placed his other forearm under her knees. She weighed very little.

"Shall we take the steps?" he asked. "Or slide down the banister?"

"Banister!" Rose demanded, while Lily giggled.

"Steps this time," Sanderly said. "Just while you're sick."

By the time they reached the foot of the stairs, Lily had lost her shyness and Rose led the way across the hall and out to the small terrace beyond. They were greeted with a cheer, and Sanderly deposited his burden on the chair next to her smallest sister who was once more bouncing with pleasure. Sanderly bowed elaborately, and would have effaced himself, had he not suddenly seen the two figures emerging around the corner.

Chapter Eleven

Harriet and Sir Ralph did not win the treasure hunt. Lady Bab and Lord Illsworth did, a mere whisker ahead of them, to a barrage of applause from those who had not taken part, and the other hunters scurrying behind them.

Harriet, laughing and clapping with everyone else was concerned to see a certain strain in Bab's demeanour. Somehow, she did not look quite delighted enough, even though she won a rather exquisite pair of earrings. Illsworth's share of the treasure was a gold and diamond cravat pin, which was quite ironic.

"Tea out here on the terrace in twenty minutes," Lady Grandison said when she and Sir John had acclaimed the winners. "There's no need to change unless you wish to!"

Harriet had no wish to, although Sir Ralph, like several other gentlemen, had got his sleeve wet by delving into the waters of the lake to retrieve the pig-skin covered clue. On the other hand, it was an excellent time to look in on the children, who had been promised their own tea on a smaller terrace near the kitchen garden. Hoping to slip away unnoticed, she hurried around the length of the house until she was surprised and slightly frustrated to find Bab at her heels.

"Are you going in to change? I'll come with you, since I don't want to find myself alone with wretched Cedric, even for an instant."

She spoke with unusual bitterness and Harriet, seeing she was genuinely upset, felt her selfish irritation melt away. "Oh dear, did something happen?"

"Well yes, he was my partner in the treasure hunt, and I kept having to swerve away from him and avoid the solitary paths, if you take my meaning. The more I see of him, the less I like him, even though we've known each other forever. Then he crept up behind me when I was reaching up for a clue in the oak tree and tried to kiss me."

"Oh, dear. Did you shame him? Or just slap him?"

"Neither," she said, blushing in a rather guilty manner. "Oh, I didn't let him, *precisely*, but as I fended him off with one hand, I felt in his pocket with the other, just in case the tie pin was there."

Harriet uttered an inappropriate choke of laughter at the picture this conjured.

"It's not funny," Bab said morosely. "He'd just worked out what I was about when James of all people caught us standing there in an embrace. Oh, Harriet, I have never seen him so livid!"

"I imagine not," Harriet said. "What happened then?"

But Bab was distracted. "He really did look rather splendid," she confided. "In fact, I was almost afraid of him. I don't know what violence he would have done to Illsworth if Snake hadn't suddenly appeared from the other side and got between them. We ladies were ordered from the scene, and the gentlemen seemed to sort it out among themselves, for they were perfectly amiable when they rejoined us, and no one had any bruises. But oh, Harriet, how am I to explain this to James? He must really believe I am at least considering a liaison with Illsworth when the truth is, I wouldn't touch him with a long-handled broom."

"Except to pick his pocket," Harriet said, and Bab let out a giggle.

"Yes, but James wouldn't believe that either. He will not even look at me, let alone speak to me, unless it is in that cold, polite voice in front of other people. Snake has vanished, so I can't ask him what went on. I don't know what to do."

"We need to think about it," Harriet said.

"Then you will help me?" Bab asked eagerly.

"If I can, but I really think you might have to resort to the truth—"

"Are we going via the kitchen?" Bab interrupted, suddenly noticing their odd direction.

"Oh, no, I'm in search of my sisters and..."

She trailed off, because they had just come in sight of the small terrace next to the kitchen garden, where a table had been set for a small tea party. Rose and Alex were laughing. Orchid was bouncing up and down on her chair while the Earl of Sanderly stepped out of the side door carrying a beaming Lily in his arms.

"What on *Earth*...?" Bab murmured, as Sanderly set Lily in the chair next to Orchid.

It was a good question. But chiefly, Harriet was aware of a rush of warmth, not just toward her family, but Sanderly, who bowed elaborately and stood back, making some remark that made all the children laugh harder, until he glanced up and saw Bab and Harriet.

His smile died instantly. That hurt, so much so that Harriet couldn't move until Bab strode forward, dragging her along.

"Harry! We thought you weren't coming!" Rose exclaimed.

"Lily wanted to come," Orchid cried, "but it was too far for her to walk, and the footmen are all busy serving tea to all of you on the big terrace. Snake had nothing better to do—"

Harriet blinked, finding her voice at last. "*Who* had nothing better to do?"

"Lord Sanderly," Orchid said meekly. "I beg your pardon. I forgot we are in public."

"Oh you needn't count me as public," said Bab, clearly thoroughly amused. "I'm only his sister."

"Miss Fforbes with two Fs?" Orchid asked.

"Mrs. Martindale with one M. But since we are on such informal terms, you had best call me Bab in private."

While this exchange had been taking place, Harriet had transferred her attention from Lily to Sanderly and finally worked out the meaning of his expression. He might really have been dismayed to see her and Bab, but only because he was embarrassed to be caught doing a kindness for the children.

"You'll forgive my interference," he drawled now. "I wouldn't have, only Orchid—" He broke off as he felt the child's anxious glare. "...and the others were eager to have their sister join them."

Another little piece of Harriet's heart melted. She knew her siblings. Orchid had been crying and now, fierce little soul, she did not want Harriet or Lily or Lady Bab to know. And Sanderly, understanding, was keeping her secret.

"I brought shawls and a blanket if Lily needs them," Rose said.

"Well done," Harriet said to her, shifting her gaze quickly to Sanderly to include him. "Thank you."

The earl was looking bored, yet his skin darkened along the fine blade of his cheekbone as though he were blushing.

"Have a cake," Orchid said, beaming at him.

"Sadly, I must leave you to your feast. Miss Cole, Bab, little Coles." He bowed and sauntered away into the house alone.

Bab was looking after him with a queer little smile on her face. She murmured something under her breath that sounded like, "Why, Snake, are you back?"

THE EVENING'S ENTERTAINMENT was to be an informal waltzing party where the young people could practice the new, rather fast dance under the watchful eyes of chaperones. The debutantes were wild with excitement. Harriet was more nervous than anything else since she knew nothing of the waltz. She barely remembered the country dances she had been taught as a child.

However, Lady Grandison summoned her and Alex to her sitting room before dinner to demonstrate. She then made Harriet and Alex take up the required positions and sang loudly with the same rhythm while they tried to waltz. Confusion and pain ensued as they danced over each other's feet and tried to go constantly in different directions. Which made them both laugh so hard that Lady Grandison began to look flustered.

"No, Harriet, you must let your partner lead. The gentlemen expect it."

"Yes, but Alex doesn't, and he has even less idea of what he's doing."

"That's a fair point," Sir John said. "I shall dance with Harriet, and you, my love, with Alex."

Since Lady Grandison continued to sing at the top of her voice, this caused Alex a fit of the giggles which quickly transferred to Harriet. Still, the dance with Sir John was something of a revelation. His hold, while strangely intimate, was utterly respectful, and it was somehow easy to dance where he led, keeping to the repetitive rhythm of the waltz.

"Much better," pronounced Lady Grandison. "You will do. Alex, you will not!"

"Thank God I'm not invited," Alex said cheekily and received a mock slap on his wrist. Sir John twinkled at him.

"Remember what we discussed," Lady Grandison said to Harriet as she was about to depart for her own room to change for the evening. "Imagine every man you dance with as your husband and see if the idea pleases you or not."

"Well, I'll try," Harriet said doubtfully, "but shouldn't I feel a little more than merely pleased with my future husband? I really don't think I would make the kind of wife gentlemen want—well, not after they realize I'm not fabulously rich."

"You'll be surprised," Lady Grandison said comfortably. "Everyone will want to dance with you. It is rude to refuse, so unless you are already promised, you must accept. I'm talking about dancing, of course. The husband is your choice."

"What if none of them will do for Harriet?" Alex asked.

"Then she has merely enjoyed the evening and knows there are lots more fish in the sea," Lady Grandison said comfortably. "You are actually quite beautiful, Harriet. You should remember that. Also, consider that once you are a well-married lady, you will be able to bring out your sisters and see them creditably established, too."

Harriet had not actually considered so far ahead, but Lily was fourteen years old. In another three years she would be of an age to be out, to be presented at court, even. She had a vision of herself and her sisters, looking much as they did now, tripping over their lace trains and squabbling their way across a room, barely remembering to curtsey to the disapproving queen.

TO HARRIET'S SECRET horror, she was placed beside Lord Illsworth for dinner. He, however, was perfectly charming, making mildly humorous conversation. He asked her to save a waltz for him, though he did not specify which, and when she thanked him, a faint frown tugged at his brow.

"I can't help feeling we have met before this party, Miss Cole."

"I should be very surprised. If we had met, I'm sure I would remember for until this week, I did not meet many strangers at all." She felt a sudden wave of homesickness and worry for all the people she had known. The tenants of the estate, the servants, the neighbours, who must all feel neglected by the family's bolt. Randolph was not a good landlord or a caring man, despite being ordained. Perhaps he would marry well and his wife would be kinder...

She dragged her mind back to the present, where Illsworth's cravat pin winked at her in the candlelight. "Congratulations on winning the treasure hunt."

"Ah, you are admiring my treasure. I owe it all to my partner Lady Bab. But we must modestly admit that you almost got there first."

"Almost does not win! You obviously had no trouble on the way."

She half-expected him to brush off the comment as meaningless, but in fact his eyes focused directly on hers for a moment.

He smiled. "Why should you imagine trouble in this idyllic setting?"

"No reason. I found the contest most good-natured, didn't you?"

"Indeed."

She could push no harder for confidences without giving away that she was helping Bab, so she resolved to wait and beard Sanderly later. With luck, he would waltz with her. For some reason that possibility caused a little tumult inside her—foolish when she liked him and was discovering more hidden kindnesses in him all the time. She also suspected him of possessing a much more sensitive soul than he showed the world. He could and was hurt by some of the barbs constantly aimed at him. His unhappiness, his loneliness, pained her, yet she always looked forward eagerly to their next encounter.

He had not been at tea on the terrace. Nor had she encountered him later in the garden with the children, or in the library. He had not appeared to see her as they gathered for dinner. At the table, his attention was divided between the scared looking debutante who had partnered James Martindale for the treasure hunt, and a spritely young matron whose name Harriet had forgotten.

Well warned by Lady Grandison, the gentlemen did not linger over their port that evening but joined the ladies in the drawing room quite promptly. Here, the carpet had been taken up and the furniture rearranged to the edges of the room, to make a dance floor. Since the dance was informal, the music was to be supplied at the pianoforte by a rota of the older matrons who had apparently been practising.

Harriet, besieged by prospective partners for the first waltz, was relieved to be able to plead her promise to Sir Ralph. She just hoped he would remember.

"I thought you had forgotten," she told him in some relief as they took the floor.

"You are understandably popular."

She placed her hand on his shoulder. "I would be flattered except I know perfectly well they all have the wrong idea about my wealth!"

Sir Ralph smiled. "Not all of them are gazetted fortune hunters, you know. Accept your success and enjoy it."

This turned out to be quite possible in Sir Ralph's company. Dancing with him took the edge off her nervousness and her fear of making clumsy mistakes. Her confidence grew, so that when he surrendered her to Mr. Dolton, she found the dance quite simple. She found it more pleasurable if she ignored her feet and relaxed. Mr. Dolton—she would not think of him as Dolt—was not as graceful as Sir Ralph, but she still followed him with ease while fending off his ardent compliments and pleas for another dance.

"Sadly, I am already promised," she said, unaware if it was even true. Since yesterday, she seemed to have promised a lot of men, although she could not remember which ones. In fact, she hoped for Sanderly, especially since he, as the most senior ranking nobleman present, had opened the party by waltzing with Lady Grandison.

She had tried not to watch, though she was left with an impression of his easy, casual grace; and her own strange, turbulent yearning. He was sitting out this second dance so perhaps he would be the first to accost her.

He wasn't.

He remained in his chair until an impromptu card game sprang up in the far corner, when he moved to take part. She danced instead with Lord Wolf, with a couple of gentlemen whose names eluded her, then Mr. Wriggley, Lord Illsworth, Mr. Poole, and a slightly older gentleman with serious dark eyes. It was all rather enjoyable, until the final waltz of the evening.

She had just sat down by Lady Grandison to catch her breath, when two gentlemen appeared, one from either side, and asked her to dance in perfect unison. Swallowing a breath of laughter, she would have refused them both, only she knew it would be rude without reason. One of them, she had certainly danced with already that evening, so she resolved to choose the other.

Before she could speak, however, Mr. Dolton said, "You've danced with him before! In which case, I must claim your prior promise!"

"And I mine," sad another indignantly.

"Ma'am, allow me to protect you from this—"

"Push off, Fool."

"Quick, Miss Cole, run away with me to the dance floor!"

"Take my hand, ma'am..."

It was quite ridiculous and tomorrow, no doubt, she would laugh about it with the children, but tension had cramped her stomach. Quite suddenly, she was transported back to the market when she was a small child, to the press of tall people and the loss of her governess. The fear of being alone in a large, noisy crowd was irrational, but it had always been with her since that long ago incident.

She turned instinctively to Lady Grandison, but she had gone. There was only this press of men, like at the inn, like at the market. A silent scream rumbled deep inside her and she was terrified it would come out. Hands were thrust in front of her face. Someone actually plucked at her right hand, then instantly someone took her left. She could not breathe.

Then abruptly, the space before her cleared. One man had elbowed several of her tormentors aside and somehow caused the others to step back from sheer force of personality. For an instant there was blessed silence, as she gazed in bewildered relief at Lord Sanderly.

He halted several paces away and slowly extended his hand. It looked like an arrogant summons, and yet she knew, she *knew*, it was an offer of aid, of relief.

She stood, closed the distance between them, and grasped his hand like a lifeline.

FOR ILLSWORTH, IT WAS like a lantern flaring in his head. This had happened before. Snake Sanderly parting a huddle of stupid, amorous young man to take their prize and kiss her.

Well, he might not be kissing her in the middle of Lady Grandison's drawing room, but surely it was the same girl? No wonder he had thought her familiar! Admittedly, he had not been entirely sober at the Duck and Spoon. He had only seen her from a distance, and her face, while gleaming with promised beauty, had been half-hidden by that ugly straw hat with the battered brim. But he was almost certain... He thought of her clear, carrying voice demanding the room she had reserved, and knew he was right.

He itched to look again at that note he had found in Sanderly's room, to decipher the signature with this new suspicion. He had time to nip up to his room and look at it before supper.

Or he could dance with the divine Bab. How much would that annoy her dull, righteous husband? To say nothing of her infernally smug brother, waltzing with the party's new darling. A darling he had already tasted, ravished and ruined.

Possibly. Right or wrong, the possibility was a powerful weapon in his hands, just when he needed one. Smiling, he strolled in Bab's direction, just as she rose and walked on to the floor with Sir Ralph.

Oh well.

Illsworth eased his way out of the drawing room and went in search of the note he had purloined. He was sure the signature would resolve quite easily now into H. Cole.

Chapter Twelve

As Sanderly's gloved fingers closed over hers, the other men muttered behind her. Harriet did not care.

She walked just a little shakily beside him to the centre of the empty dance floor.

Why is no one else here?

As though she had asked aloud, Sanderly answered. "Your—er...suitors were so busy competing with each other, that they are only now making a dash to find other partners who will almost all feel insulted. Everyone else was too busy gawping at the indecent scene around you."

Other couples were walking onto the floor at last, so she did not feel quite so exposed.

"I'm sorry," she whispered. "I did not handle it well. There were just suddenly so many of them, so close... It reminded me—" She broke off for his eyelids swept down suddenly.

At the pianoforte, Lady Grandison began to play the introduction. *So that is where she went.* Harriet did not exactly jump when Sanderly's arm encircled her waist, his hand resting lightly at her back, but it felt like a jolt of electricity, causing her breath to catch in shock. She laid her fingers very warily, very lightly on his shoulder.

"It reminded you of the inn," he said tonelessly, although she glimpsed an odd bleakness in his eyes.

"Oh, no," she blurted. "Actually, you saved me from that too, because it was just beginning when you shooed them all away."

"What was just beginning?"

"My foolish panic. When I was very small, I got lost in a busy market and was foolishly frightened amongst all the noise and the press of people, and when they noticed and tried to be kind to me and find out who I was with, it was even worse because they all spoke at once and I could not understand any of them, just that they were strangers pulling me this way and that, and there were so many of them I could not *breathe*."

At some point during her tale, they had begun to dance. It began so smoothly she had barely been aware of it for the shame of her confession. She merely followed him blindly, instinctively. Now she realized how wonderful it felt, moving and turning with him in perfect unison. She had never felt so graceful, so...

Oh goodness, I am drowning in those eyes. No man should have eyes so very beautiful... "You knew about my stupid upset, didn't you? Both times."

"I used it," he corrected. "Particularly the first time. I believe I really do apologize for the assault."

"It was nothing," she said dismissively, even while heat crept into her face. "Just a kiss."

To her surprise, laughter blazed into his eyes, lightening his whole face. "A knock-out blow, Miss Cole. I concede."

"To what? What did I say?"

"However ill he behaves, no man likes his attentions to be described as *nothing* or *just a kiss*. Even if you are angry, we expect you to be secretly overwhelmed with pleasure and gratitude."

Harriet, whose memory of the kiss was so vivid that she could almost feel it now on her mouth, said hastily, "At all events, you dance excellently. I have forgotten I never waltzed before this evening."

"My self-respect is restored."

She laughed and he spun her around to the music. A sense of magic began to creep over her, a happiness that had no cause except the man who held her, who brought this physical exhilaration she had never experienced in dancing. They talked occasionally, with touches of humour and fun, but mostly she just *felt* and wished the dance could go on forever.

This is the happiest I will ever be...

"It is ending," he said at last. "Shall I take you in to supper or restore you to your godmother? Or even my sister who will probably keep you safe."

She could not bear it to end. She did not want to be with anyone else.

"I believe I would appreciate a little fresh air."

"To avoid the first crush of the dining room."

"Yes," she said gratefully, although it was not true. "Besides, it is not so long since we dined."

She supposed he was practiced at slipping quietly away from crowds with the woman of his choice. Somehow that didn't matter either. Only being with him mattered. No one else here would advise her to trust him. And yet she did.

Mingling with the crowd, somehow never letting them get too close, he guided her in the vague direction of Lady Grandison, then quietly through the adjoining door to the garden room.

As the door closed behind her, she was in darkness. Removing her hand from his arm, he held it and drew her forward as though he could see perfectly well. Perhaps he could, for they bumped into nothing. She was barely aware of her surroundings, only of *him*.

A curtain swished and moonlight shone through the glass. A bolt slid back and a breeze stirred her hair as she stepped outside onto the terrace.

Still he held her hand and she was too happy to withdraw it. They stood very close together, gazing upward at the moon, at the silver glow it cast over the terraced lawns and the lake beyond, at the gently rustling trees on the other side.

Her ears sang with silence. His warmth invaded her, his clean, masculine scent of citrus and earth beguiled her. A strange, delicious weakness was seeping through her, and yet along with it came desperate longing, a need so powerful that she didn't know what to do with it.

"Better?" he asked, his voice soft as ever, yet oddly husky. Could he feel it too, this magic, this wonder?

Of course he does not. He is a man of the world who has known a hundred women. He only feels sorry for me, and perhaps ashamed.

She didn't want him to be ashamed.

"Much better," she replied. Her heart thundered in her breast as though trying to beat its way out.

Involuntarily, she tightened her grip on his hand and felt his thumb glide across her palm in an absent caress. Or did he mean it? Probably not, for he made no move to take her in his arms. When had his mere company become not enough? Despite what everyone thought of him, he was too kind, too honourable, to take advantage of her.

"I didn't mind, you know," she blurted.

At least he turned his head to look at her. By the light of the moon and the candlelight seeping from the drawing room windows, she could make out the sharp bones and deep hollows of his cheeks, the glittering of his ridiculously beautiful eyes.

"Mind what?"

"Your kissing me. I know I should, because you only did it to be insolent and annoy your friends, and to secretly give me your key to be safe, which was extraordinarily kind. But I regard it as a new experience. No one has ever kissed me before like that."

"Then is the matter done with?" he asked softly. "Or would you like to experience it again?"

She swallowed. "Again, if you please."

His lips quirked. He turned toward her, raising her hand which he placed on his shoulder before tipping up her chin with one gloved finger. He bent his head slowly, giving her time to escape, perhaps, but she only parted her lips in anticipation. She felt his quickened breath on her cheek, her chin, caught a hint of wine...

Oh God, do it, kiss me!

She would have reached up to press her lips to his, if only to break the tension, only she was afraid of ruining the moment.

If the moment ever came.

"You are too sweet," he said huskily. "I should not touch you."

"You are touching me," she pointed out. *Stupid, stupid...*

His lips curved in his rare, genuine smile, laughing at her perhaps, but she did not care for his mouth finally touched hers, a soft, gentle glide that deprived her of breath and made her stomach leap. Then she gasped as his warm hand closed around her nape—when had he removed his glove?—and his mouth fastened, soft and gentle and utterly devastating.

It was nothing like the kiss at the inn, which had been insolent, arrogant. This one *gave*, caressed and coaxed. In wonder, she let him explore with his lips, even kissed him back. Her whole stomach melted into delicious weakness. Deep, sensual pleasure flowed through her from his mouth into hers. The touch of his tongue, the slow, invasive caress of his lips...

The kiss grew stronger, deeper. The touch of his body sent flame licking through her. She slid her hand from his shoulder to his nape, grasping at his hair. And still he kissed her, on and on. And she kissed him back with every instinct she possessed, praying it would never end.

It had to, of course, if only to let them draw breath. When his mouth finally released hers, she seemed to have difficulty opening her eyes, afraid she had dreamed the whole thing. But no, his warmth was still here. His arm lay solidly at her back, his fingers still now on her neck, his chest against her breasts. She fluttered her eyelids open, and there were his amazing eyes, fixed on hers with an unguarded expression that looked like...bewilderment.

He raised his head, his lashes closing down like a veil, while slowly enough for it to appear reluctant, he loosened his arms and dropped them to his side.

"Well," he said. "An experience for us both. I assure you I will treasure mine. You had best go back alone. I don't believe I have upset your hair or your gown—such astonishing restraint on my part—though I would seize some lemonade to cool your rosy lips. Goodnight, Miss Cole."

Dismissed.

It was not obedience that turned her away from him. It was sudden pain and a kind of stunned indignation. He had reduced the beauty of their moment back to the insolence of the inn, which at least she knew how to deal with. She might not have the key to his room this time, but she knew how to walk away.

And yet as she did so, head high, with deliciously tingling lips and devastation in her heart, she knew it was he who was really walking away.

SANDERLY HATED HIMSELF.

He was used to that, though not to the strength and fury of this surge. He had known not to touch her, not after that first time at the inn had unnerved him. And yet, like a fool, he had given in to it just because she wanted it. Because she *liked* him.

Idiot. The girl was nineteen years old, though she might as well have been Lily's age for all the experience she had of the world. She probably thought he would marry her now, but dear God, she did not deserve that fate.

He had to get away from here. Africa had never shouted so loudly. Time to pack. Again.

Only, he still couldn't. Because of Bab and her damned mess and the duel that had seemed her only way out. Perhaps Grandison and

Martindale would sort out some reconciliation between them, though they would have to find a way that still spiked Illsworth's guns.

Could that be done with threats and oaths and solicitors' letters? He had better find James and direct him. Then, with luck, he could be gone in the morning, and never trouble Harriet Cole again.

But *she* had troubles that did not involve him. She had unspeakable Cousin Randolph, and her only honourable escape from him—as she saw it—drudgery in a school that may or may not agree to house and educate her sisters.

These thoughts took him twice around the outside of the house at high speed. He re-entered via the small terrace where the children had had tea and into the main hall. He strode purposefully toward the staircase, where he met Grandison coming down.

Sanderly did not expect people to look pleased to see him, and Grandison didn't.

Sanderly bowed slightly. "I wonder if you could spare me a few minutes of your time, sir?"

Grandison scowled. "I have already given enough of my time this evening to the nonsense of this duel, and I have no desire to waste any more."

"Actually, it isn't about the duel, though I apologize for that. It seemed the only solution, as I hope Martindale has already explained to you."

Grandison regarded him with some suspicion, for he had forgotten to drawl and sneer. There seemed to be no time for such charades.

"Come into my study," Sir John said abruptly and stalked across the hall, leaving Sanderly to trail after him.

The study, revealed as Grandison lit the nearest lamp and turned it up, was a small but comfortable room with a desk and chair, shelves full of ledgers and pamphlets, and two comfortable leather armchairs which Grandison indicated with a gesture of one hand.

Sanderly sat.

"Brandy?" Grandison said, sloshing liquid from an old decanter into two glasses without waiting for a reply.

"Thank you," Sanderly said politely, which earned him another glance of suspicion.

"Martindale told me about the insult to his wife, your sister. I never realized Illsworth was such a scoundrel, and I quite understand the necessity of discreet satisfaction. However, I will tell you what I told Martindale. I will not have my wife's hospitality abused in such a way. You must take your quarrel elsewhere. Though you may be assured Illsworth will not be invited or received again."

"Your friends are your own business, sir. I would not presume to interfere. And I shall meet Illsworth beyond the boundary of your land if you tell me precisely where that is."

"For such a purpose, the boundary is imaginary," Grandison snapped. "The world will know the quarrel began here at Grand Court."

Sanderly took a sip of brandy. "The world need not know at all. I don't propose to make the event something Illsworth will ever brag about, and the discretion of Martindale and myself is assured. I regret I cannot offer you more than that if I am to shut Illsworth's malicious mouth before I leave the country."

Grandison frowned. "I have just given you the best excuse I can not to fight him at all. Am I to understand you do not *wish* me to reconcile you?"

Sanderly twisted his lips. "Is that what you thought I wanted of you? What a paltry fellow I am. No, my business with you is quite other. Well, strictly speaking it is not my business at all. I understand Miss Cole is your wife's goddaughter. She appears to be a somewhat quixotic creature, so I am not certain she has explained to you or your wife precisely how her cousin has behaved toward her family."

"Precisely? No. But I know enough. What is your interest, my lord?"

"Oh, I have none. I merely have a quite uncharacteristic dislike of bullies, and I am fairly sure this Randolph is one such creature. I am equally certain that he is abusing his position, probably with more than mere unkindness as his motive, and that the involvement of solicitors in their affairs would be beneficial to Miss Cole and her family."

"I have already written to my solicitors," Grandison said stiffly. "I believe I know my duty to my wife's goddaughter."

Sanderly leaned forward and set his glass down on the desk. "In that case, I shall trouble you no further on the matter. I propose to be out of your hair by the day after tomorrow. Unless you can persuade Martindale—and Illsworth—that the involvement of solicitors in keeping his lordship's malicious person away from my sister is also better than duelling. If you manage that—and I am aware it is a tall order—your reward will be my departure a day early." He rose and bowed. "My thanks for your time. Good evening."

Chapter Thirteen

"What's the matter?" Lily asked the following morning as Harriet, washed and dressed, gazed out of their bedchamber window.

Harriet turned quickly to face her. Lily looked somehow brighter than yesterday, still pale and not exactly rested despite her long sleep, but her eyes were less dull, and she was obviously paying more attention.

"Nothing new," Harriet said lightly. Which was not remotely true. She just had no idea how to explain it to her sister. She wanted to say, *I think I have fallen in love with Lord Sanderly. He kissed me last night and it was so wonderful...*

And there, she ran out of clarity. Could a man kiss like that and not mean it even a little? Yet having made her feel...*that*, he had sent her back inside as if she had failed some simple test.

She must have disappointed him.

Or shocked him by her forwardness. She had all but flung herself into his arms, after all. But then there had been that look in his eyes, tender and yet bewildered, almost desperately so...

It was all ridiculously confusing, and she didn't know whether she was deliriously happy or tragically sad.

If he leaves...

He would leave. In his heart, he had already gone.

The clip-clop of a horse on the flags below dragged her attention back to the window and caught at her breath, because it was Lord Sanderly himself, mounted on a large grey horse. The animal trotted briskly toward the bridle path and the woods. Its rider did not look back at the house. In fact, they broke into a canter. There was no way she could catch up with him.

So much for her hope of coming across him during another early morning walk.

He did not want to see her. Pain clawed at her heart. She had thought they were friends, at least.

She swung back to Lily, forcing a smile to her lips. "Are you hungry? Shall we have breakfast early? I'm sure the others are awake."

SANDERLY RETURNED FROM his ride, satisfied with his achievement. He breakfasted with several of the guests who did their best to civilly ignore him. Illsworth, sitting beside Alicia Eldridge smiled blandly at him as though to point out that if their duel was public, it was Illsworth who would have everyone's support.

Well aware of it, Sanderly smiled back with as much of a sneer as he could muster. He was so damned tired of this. He wanted to be away from this life, these people. Even Harriet Cole. *Especially* Harriet Cole.

At least she was not present. He gathered she broke her fast with the children. Which would be considerably more enjoyable.

Bab entered the room with her usual bright good morning. But there were shadows of strain around her eyes. She was not sleeping well. James rose politely, as did the other gentlemen, but as she began choosing from the dishes on the sideboard, he excused himself with a bow and left the parlour.

Idiot. Sanderly finished his coffee and left in a more leisurely fashion. Only Grandison acknowledged his bow, though Wolf, encountered at the door, did cast him a distracted grin.

Sanderly discovered James alone in the library, an impressive room with an even more impressive collection of books.

"Ah, there you are," Sanderly greeted him. "Avoiding your wife for the edification of the gossips?"

James flushed slightly. "I treat my wife with every courtesy."

"I treat Illsworth with courtesy. What does that prove?"

"What do you want, Sanderly?" James said impatiently.

"I have discovered a suitable site for the duel, on a patch of common ground at the edge of the woodland, just beyond Grandison's boundary. It does not appear to be in use, even for grazing. Here, I'll show you." He took the map he had purloined earlier from these shelves and spread it on the table beside James.

James grunted. "As good as anywhere. I have an appointment with Grandison later this morning to discuss the matter. Tomorrow at dawn, pistols, twenty paces. Damn it, I wish you'd let *me* kill him."

Sanderly blinked. "Hitherto quite unsuspected thirst for blood," he remarked. "We've discussed why it cannot be you."

"Are you going to kill him?" James asked.

"Of course not. Which is why we are not choosing pistols but swords. First blood will be sufficient."

James stared at him with surprise and just a little contempt. "*Swords*? Who the devil fights with swords in this day and age?"

"Soldiers," Sanderly said gently.

James's eyes widened, as though he had forgotten that Sanderly had ever been a soldier.

"Quite," Sanderly said. "Be sure Grandison reminds Illsworth of the fact. Recall that I was once an excellent soldier and mentioned in dispatches for my victorious charge at Salamanca with—er... swords. I want him frightened."

James no longer disguised his disgust. "You want him to withdraw."

"I do. By keeping the duel between ourselves, we have made that easy for him. We will make acceptance of his apology dependent upon certain conditions, even a legally signed paper—I'm still mulling details—that will keep him out of Bab's life."

James curled his lip. "And yours."

"Oh, *well* out of mine. I shan't even be in the country."

"Why don't you go today and remove all risk to yourself?" James said with disdain.

"Dear James, I would if only I could rely on you not to make a mess of this as well as of my sister's life."

James sprang to his feet. "She chooses him over me at every opportunity! And if you recall, it was not I who was discovered in the arms of another!"

"Be grateful," said Sanderly. "You, I probably *would* have killed. For sheer stupidity if for nothing else. Could you really not see that Bab was an unwilling captive?"

"Then how did she get into the situation in the first place?"

Sanderly contemplated him. "I suspect she was looking for something and misjudged. Again."

"Looking for what?" James asked wearily.

"The same thing as you," Sanderly said on impulse. He was rewarded by the faintest widening of his brother-in-law's eyes, a tiny movement of one foot.

"I don't know what you're talking about."

"And if you did, you still wouldn't tell so paltry a creature as me. I understand. Just scare Illsworth and bring me his apology. By the time you do, I shall have all the necessary conditions committed to paper for his signature before you and Grandison. And then, thank God, I can shake the dust of this benighted place from my gleaming Hoby boots."

ILLSWORTH WAS CLEANING his duelling pistols and congratulating himself on his forethought in bringing them with him. They were gold-mounted and rather beautiful, a gift from his father on his twenty-first birthday, and he had been loath to sell them, although that was his intention. On his departure from Grand Court, he would call upon a collector who had offered him an excellent price.

Which he might not need to consider anymore. If he could secure Harriet Cole in marriage, he thought dreamily, his financial troubles would be over.

A knock at the door interrupted his self-satisfied musings. Hastily, he shoved the pistols, brush, cloth and oil, into the drawer of his desk.

"Enter."

Sir John Grandison came in, brisk but frowning. In their uncomfortable interview last night, Grandison had left him in no doubt of his opinion of this duel, although he had at least agreed that Sanderly was unmanageable and at fault to goad him to such a degree. Neither of them had criticised Lady Bab.

Illsworth rose. "Ah, Sir John. Please, sit down. Have you news?"

"Yes, but you're not going to like it." Grandison sat down heavily in the nearer of the two arm chairs. "Sanderly has chosen swords."

Illsworth felt his jaw drop and reclaimed it. "*Swords?*"

"Swords. Can you fence?"

"I had lessons at school. Fifteen years ago!"

"Sanderly's sword experience is somewhat more recent, though rather more brutal than gentlemanly fencing. But the good news is, Sanderly is not opposed to receiving your apology. I'm sure we can word it so that—"

"I have no intention of apologizing to that misbegotten coward," Illsworth interrupted.

Grandison held his gaze. "Why not? You were caught assaulting his sister."

"It was no assault, Grandison. She threw herself at me. She's an incorrigible flirt, and who can blame her with such a dull stick for a husband?"

"And yet you challenged Sanderly."

"I told you: his insults were insupportable. *Tha*t is our quarrel, nothing to do with his sister. So the apology should come from him."

"What do you want him to say?"

"I want him to withdraw every word he spoke to me yesterday afternoon."

"And if he doesn't?"

The idea of swords had panicked Illsworth just at first, because he had not thought of them, and Sanderly was a veteran of several battles before he lost his nerve. But it was unlikely that he had truly found that nerve again. These days, all his fighting was done with his damned nasty tongue. Apart from a spot of ungentlemanly strangling, Illsworth recalled indignantly, which had taken him by surprise. Besides, with any weapon, there were ways to win, especially in such a private affair as this one.

He might lose Bab, but his way would be clear to Harriet Cole's fortune.

"Then I shall meet him," Illsworth said dismissively. "I would like to do the world a favour and remove him from it, but—"

"First blood ends it," Sir John snapped.

"As you command," Illsworth said blandly. One chance was all he needed.

THE AFTERNOON'S ENTERTAINMENT was boating upon the lake. But any hopes Harriet harboured of being rowed by Lord Sanderly were dashed at the outset by Lady Grandison's greeting.

"Ah, Harriet! You look pretty. I've put you with Lord Illsworth today."

This was not good news, for she did not like the man, but she could do nothing but smile and accept his lordship's arm. By chance, she glanced at Sir John and caught an expression on his face of pure exasperation.

With perfect courtesy, Illsworth escorted her to their assigned boat, jumped nimbly in and reached up to help her.

The lake looked very pretty with all these small, brightly painted boats dotted about the water. The plan was to laze around the lake for a little and then race from one end of the lake to the other. Harriet could see Sanderly in the distance. He seemed to be doing more floating than rowing. Was the lady with him more to his taste than she was? He had clearly moved on from Mrs. Eldridge, although perhaps she had moved on from him, influenced by the general ill-feeling toward him. Was he hurt?

She doubted his heart had been involved in the first place. He had not looked at her...*so*. Not the way he had looked at Harriet.

Oh, who are you fooling? she lashed herself. *He does not want you, you were entirely mistaken.*

And yet, I want him still. Have I no pride?

"*That* is where I saw you before," Illsworth said suddenly, causing her to blink at him in surprise. Up until now he had made gentle, unthreatening conversation that required little response.

"In a boat?" she said, trailing her fingers through the water. "I don't believe I have ever been in one before. It is rather pleasant."

"It is," he agreed, "but no, it wasn't in a boat I saw you."

She raised her eyebrows, trying to appear merely curious, even though her heart beat with sudden dread that he was about to ruin her reputation with three words: *Duck and Spoon*.

"A posting inn," he said, smiling. "But which one?"

"I cannot imagine."

"It will come to me."

It had come to him already. He knew. Something about his manner reminded her of a cat playing with a mouse. She tried to control the surge of panic, of sheer embarrassment.

"No doubt." She allowed a hint of boredom into her voice and gazed up at the clouds which had grown thicker and darker than the last time she looked. "Do you know, I think we shall be caught in the rain."

"Then let us row to the starting point and hope we can beat the rain as well as our opponents."

To her alarm, he began to row rather more strongly, sweeping past the other boats, pulling further away from them and the watchers on the bank, heading for the starting point at the other end of the lake.

Warily, she kept her gaze on his face. They were still within sight of everyone else, but she could not help her feeling of threat. Trapped in a boat with him, in a dreadful kind of privacy, what kind of insult would she face?

As if noticing her fixed gaze, he smiled. "Is everything well, Miss Cole?"

"Perfectly," she replied. "I hope you have not used all your strength getting to this point or we shall struggle in the race."

"Just practising, I assure you. And now I have the best starting position, I can rest while the others tire themselves catching up. Did I tell you how delightful you look this afternoon? I believe that is why I took so long to recognize you."

"I did not look delightful when you think you last saw me?"

Illsworth considered. "Yes, you did. In a frumpy, ragged kind of way one does not associate at all with Lady Grandison's connections."

Harriet laughed, gazing longingly at the other boats, most of which were now working their way up toward them. In the lead, she recognized Sanderly's dark head and felt better, even though he did not appear to be exerting himself.

She said, "Have you considered that it was not me at all?"

"I always consider everything, Miss Cole. Are you involved in this evening's dramatics?"

Their entertainment tonight was to be a play performed by a group of guests who had been practising all week.

She shook her head. "No, it is the guests who arrived first who are involved, I believe. But I shall enjoy watching."

"Perhaps you would care to enjoy it with me?"

There was little she would care for less, but to snub him would be rude. Besides, pride would not allow her to let him think he had rattled her. "How kind."

"Not remotely. I suspect your company will be all that makes the evening bearable, though I beg you will not tell our amateur thespians I said so."

"I would not dream of it," she assured him. She could not work out if he was flirting with her or threatening her in some subtle way she could not grasp. His change of subject confused her and there was a sort of softened yet greedy look in his eyes that she did not like.

Was it possible that he too was courting her for her imaginary fortune? Even while pursuing Lady Bab? Though it was possible Bab's husband and brother had put a stop to that during their private chat yesterday afternoon.

Either way, the idea made her uneasy, if not downright queasy. If he was courting her, why hint at the Duck and Spoon? To show he did not care?

A spot of rain landed on her upturned face. She realized the sky had darkened even more, and as far as the eye could see. The heavens were surely about to open, and the deluge had never been more welcome.

"Hurry!" someone called from the approaching boats. "We're about to get soaked!"

"We'll manage the race if we start in the next couple of minutes," Illsworth said.

Lady Grandison, bustling up to the starting point, waved everyone hurriedly into place and dropped her handkerchief. Illsworth pulled hard on the oars and their boat surged ahead while rain began to patter on Harriet's newly borrowed hat.

Some squeals of protest came from ladies in other boats. Footmen hurried along the near bank of the lake with umbrellas for the watchers. But the race quickly disintegrated in the downpour which soaked rowers and passengers and threatened to fill up the boats.

"Sadly, I must give up being your champion this afternoon," Illsworth said as Lord Sanderly's boat cut across their path, making with all haste for the bank. Sanderly's passenger was the quiet debutante who was covering her head with her arms, as though that could possibly make her less wet. Neither of them glanced at Harriet or Illsworth.

Harriet nodded. She had rarely been so relieved, and she was more than happy to get soaked to avoid the rest of her time with Illsworth.

The outdoor servants, armed with long-handled boat hooks, were helping drag boats faster into the shore and hand out the intrepid sailors, all of whom hared off immediately in the direction of the house.

"Quite a show for a seafaring nation," murmured Sanderly's amused voice behind Harriet as she stumbled ashore with a servant's aid. She glanced around eagerly, but of course, he was not talking to her but to the quiet debutante whom he sheltered with his coat. "Nelson would be proud."

He did not look at her. Illsworth's arm swept her forward toward the house. He snatched an umbrella from a hurrying footman and threw it up. Harriet kept a smile on her face because the dash in the rain should have been fun. It would have been fun, had she been with Sanderly, who now would not look at her.

"Tea in the drawing room in twenty minutes!" Lady Grandison called to all. "So hurry and change into dry clothes! The fires will be lit to warm you..."

Harriet fled.

She found Lily waking up after yet another nap. She was dressed, though lying on her bed with the coverlet over her.

"Goodness, is it raining?"

"No, I jumped in the lake."

Lily giggled, a welcome sound. "You look as if you did. You'd better get out of those things or you'll catch cold. Let me help..."

"You will help by sitting up and putting that shawl around you. Ugh, I am soaked quite to the skin."

She had only just dressed in yet another different gown and was hanging up the wet things to dry as best they could, when the children all but burst into the room. Mildred was with them, looking harassed.

"It was him!" Orchid was all but yelling as she stamped in. "I saw him! Harriet, we can't stay here any longer."

"Oh dear, why not?" Harriet asked calmly, well-used to her smallest sister's ways.

"Because Cousin Randolph has found us!"

Chapter Fourteen

"*What?*" Harriet swung on her with considerably more attention. "Randolph is *here*? At Grand Court?"

"No, he isn't," Alex scoffed.

"He is!" Orchid cried. "I saw him today at the inn!"

"No one else did," Rose said wryly. "And we were all together. I think she might have seen someone who looked a bit like Randolph, and it gave her a fright."

Harriet looked doubtfully around them all.

"It *was* him," Orchid said stubbornly.

"Why would he be at the inn?" Alex asked reasonably. "If he was looking for us, he would have come here."

"I really don't think he'll be looking for us at all," Harriet said. It was a sensible conclusion reached in the safety of Grand Court. Her earlier insistence on secrecy now seemed silly. "He will be so glad to be rid of us that he'll do nothing." Of course, he had lost his housekeeper and unpaid servants, but he finally had the house to himself, and he would not be troubled by old servants or tenants who addressed her and the children as if they were still lords of the manor and Randolph some minor connection. He had been trying to drive them out and he had succeeded.

"Was this at the village inn?" she asked.

"Yes, miss," Mildred said, speaking for the first time. "I took them to the village shop with me and then we stopped for a drink at the inn, and just as we were leaving, the child set up this screech and made us all hide."

"Did you see this man who frightened her?"

"No, miss. There was a carriage, but I didn't see any passenger, only the coachman who was muffled up to the ears. The rain had started by then."

"It will have been the coachman she saw," Rose said.

"It wasn't," Orchid muttered.

"Whoever it was," Mildred said hastily, "I couldn't persuade her to go back into the inn until the rain went off, so we're soaked through and need to change."

"To the nursery with you," Harriet commanded. "Come! Orchid, stop fretting. Even if it was Randolph—"

"It was!"

"You have nothing to fear from him. We're Lady Grandison's guests here."

"Sir John will see him off," Alex said, catching on.

Orchid's hand crept into Harriet's. "He will, won't he? And Lord Snake will too."

Harriet no longer knew what Lord Sanderly would do. He appeared to be avoiding her, though whether for the sake of her reputation or because he regretted their kiss last night, she had no idea. Even worse, had he just forgotten? That thought made her cringe inside.

SANDERLY HAD NOT FORGOTTEN.

Not by a long chalk, and it made escape more urgent than ever. He was therefore eager to receive his brother-in-law when James knocked on his bedchamber door shortly before dinner.

"What news?" Sanderly asked, by way of greeting as their eyes met in the looking glass.

"Bad," James replied in his precise way. "Illsworth will not play our game. He has agreed to swords and he will not apologize. I think you misjudged him."

It was possible. Once, the lives of his men and his comrades had depended on his accurate judgement of character. He had imagined he was good at it. And he had been wrong.

He placed his cravat pin and reached for his coat. "I was at school with Illsworth. He was manipulative and used others to fight his battles. He cheats at cards and uses loaded dice."

James sat down heavily. "My lord, those are serious accusations."

Sanderly curled his lip. "Are they?"

James blushed. Presumably he had forgotten that such accusations had been levelled at Sanderly continuously during the last year.

"You think it an irrelevant observation to the present matter," Sanderly said carelessly. "But it isn't. Illsworth is not used to fighting his own battles and he cheats. But he is not stupid. I think he has rumbled us."

"Rumbled us?"

Sanderly fastened his coat, inspecting himself in the glass. "He knows I want an apology and takes it as cowardice. He thinks I will find another way to cry off."

"*I* should be the one fighting him," James said with unwonted savagery. "Why did you intervene? Why did I let you?"

"Who knows? Perhaps, just for an instant you imagined I would punish him more safely. God forbid, and I'm sure it won't happen again, but you might actually have trusted me. Shall we go down to dinner, since you appear to have abandoned my sister once more?"

James rose absently, frowning at Sanderly. "Wait! What do you intend to do?"

"Meet him tomorrow as agreed. If I fail, you may then, of course, murder him however you wish and face the hangman. At least Bab will be able to marry again. I hope she chooses someone with more wits next time, though the scandal of a hanged husband might scupper her chances."

"You needn't be so damned offensive!"

Sanderly met his gaze. "Need I not?" His voice was as soft and sardonic as usual, and yet James seemed to perceive something that pulled him up short, for a sudden frown marred his brow and he did not at once move.

"I am aware some people are offensive when they speak of you," James said with rare difficulty. "I hope you know *I* have never spoken so."

Sanderly nodded. "For Bab's sake. I am aware. I have not yet sunk so low as to thank you for it. She is your wife after all. She is impulsive and even foolish at times, but her feelings are deep and her nature loyal. If you really don't know that by now, I must have been right in the first place to refuse the match."

James swallowed hard. "She does not trust me."

"You don't trust her."

"She gave away my first gift!"

Sanderly paused, his hand grasping the door handle. So James knew... "And she has been trying to get it back ever since. In a rage, one does foolish things. And pays for them. You will look after my sister. I have made adequate financial arrangements for all eventualities. The rest is up to you." He opened the door. "Don't dawdle, James. You'll need a hearty meal before you face the evening's dramatics. To say nothing of the morning's."

⁂

TWELVE MORE HOURS AND I shall be gone.

The words repeated in his head throughout the evening, with yearning, yet not with happiness. He could not remember the last time he had been happy.

Yes he could. Last night, with Harriet Cole in his arms, her sweet, trusting, unskilled kiss on his lips.

Sitting alone at the back of the ballroom, he pretended to watch the play on the makeshift stage. It was amusing enough, largely because of the hilarity of the performers and their enthusiastic delivery of lines they frequently forgot. In reality he was watching Harriet, who sat several rows in front of him beside Illsworth. That was a development he did not like. There was little point in delivering Bab from his clutches if he already had his claws into Harriet.

Harriet who was *not* his responsibility yet felt strangely like his only friend.

Oh, but there was passion in her. More than that, she had *feelings*, depth, decency, compassion, humour, loyalty... all the things he had once valued.

If she stayed in Society, she would soon learn to despise him. If she ever thought of him.

I will think of her.

I will learn not to. When I escape and am lost in other countries, other people, other beauty.

He had known her a mere few days after all. And yet she liked him. Not his wicked reputation or damning tongue, nor the promise of his loveless skills in the bedchamber which were the only reason women usually tolerated him. He was bored taking advantage of that, weary of resentment and...

He was not weary of *her*. Nor she of him. She was a glimmer of... *hope*.

And for that, he owed her...something. His absence, certainly, but perhaps also a farewell. He did not want her to be hurt, to lose her trusting nature.

Abruptly, he remembered the children. The fragile Lily, the curious, fun-loving younger ones. They had seemed to like him, too. *How odd...*

The play finished to uproarious applause and a great deal of laughter. The actors took their exaggerated bows.

Amongst the audience, Harriet appeared to be excusing herself to Illsworth, which gave Sanderly an instant's relief. She was in little danger of being beguiled by him. She was, after all, in Bab's confidence. As for Illsworth, who would lose interest as soon as he discovered her fortune was modest, his sting should be drawn tomorrow.

All the same, when Harriet went in the opposite direction to her aunt's, and slipped out of the ballroom, Sanderly followed.

He was fairly sure she was going to look in on her siblings and had no intention of allowing Illsworth or one of her other admirers to waylay her en route. This was his only chance to make things...if not right, then at least easier for her.

He had been cheerfully and indiscriminately hurting the feelings of people all year. Was it good or bad that he had not yet sunk so low as to hurt her more than he had to?

She ran lightly up the ballroom stairs which led to the back of the entrance hall, and then headed for the staircase. Then, no doubt hearing his footfall, she stopped and whirled around to face him.

"Oh, it's you," she said in relief. "I was just going to see Lily, and then the children."

"How is Lily?"

"The doctor believes she is not ill, merely convalescing. With rest and good food, she should recover fully. Certainly, there has been no recurrence of the fever." She did not rush away from him as she should. Though her eyes were anxious, there was no fear, no distaste, just uncertainty. He had taken liberties last night and then dismissed her, for her sake as much as for his own.

"I was going to the library," he said, gesturing toward the staircase. The hall was empty, the guests enjoying a light supper in the ballroom. They walked up together, not touching. In spite of himself, something soared inside him when she turned her step toward the library with him. "I'm glad I ran into you. I shall be leaving early, so I wanted to say goodbye now."

Her gaze flew to his. "Leaving?"

She was dismayed. He heard it in her voice, saw it in her eyes. It caused an ache he couldn't locate. "I have always been leaving. It is high time I got around to it."

"But...but Bab—"

"Bab's difficulties should be solved by tomorrow."

"You have found the pin?"

"If our friend has it, it will be returned. The rest is between Bab and James." He forgot to say *dear* James. "You will give my regards to your family? And please take my advice and do not be kind to the inestimable Cousin Randolph."

"Oh. Orchid claims she saw him."

Entering the library behind her, he paused, distracted from the short, kind speech he had been about to make. "Randolph? Where?"

She paused at the first table, where a book lay open. There was enough light from the lamp to read it by, and she picked it up almost mechanically, inspecting the title and running her small, slender fingers over the spine. "At the village inn, but none of the others saw him. I think it is her fear of him colouring her imagination."

"Trust Sir John," he said abruptly. Leaving the door open, he followed her and stood with the table between them.

"I do," she said with a hint of impatience. "And her ladyship. In fact, I believe we had no need of secrecy. As long as we do not blacken his name, Randolph will simply be grateful we are gone. Why are you leaving?"

"I should not be here at all. I was invited for form's sake and declined as expected. I only came to see what Bab wanted."

"And missed your ship."

"There will be another."

She stared at him. There was a desperate hurt in her eyes, but also bewilderment. "You are letting them drive you from your own country, your own estates and responsibilities."

"I drive myself. No one will suffer."

She set the book down with unnecessary force. "Why? Can't you be truthful for once?"

That stung, mainly because she was right. His whole life was lies, his own and the world's. And now this girl accused him with her eyes and her words, her anger and disappointment and something terribly like longing. He swung away from her, meaning to sneer and mock, but she spoke again first.

"*Why?*"

And quite suddenly, something snapped. "Because my life is *unbearable*! *I* am unbearable."

She had moved, damn her, to stand facing him, the table no longer between them.

"Not to me," she whispered.

He saw the effort it cost her. The girl had pride and yet the courage to leave herself open to the hurt she knew he would inflict. She was offering herself—in what capacity he did not know and doubted she did either—which not only stunned him. It scared him.

"Because you don't know me," he said with contempt.

It should have frightened her off, in high dudgeon, too, but to his astonishment she reached out and took his hand, and the rest of his blistering speech died unspoken.

She gazed into his eyes. "What happened?"

"When?" he asked blankly.

"One man went to war. Another came home."

Who had told her that? How could she know?

"What happened?" she repeated.

"My brother died." The words spilled out without permission. And then, it seemed, he could not stop. "I had seen men die. Some of them were friends I would have died to save. I thought I knew death, imagined I could deal with it. But I could not deal with Hugo's. He was not a soldier. He was young and healthy and he died, and nothing made sense anymore. I told no one when I heard. I just got vilely drunk and played cards with my fellow officers. It was one of those periods of inaction and boredom and waiting. If there had been orders, battles to fight, even marching to do, I might have... But I didn't. I behaved badly. Someone said I cheated—"

"Did you?"

"God knows. If I did, it was by accident, a dropped card I'd forgotten about because I was so damned drunk. I beg your pardon."

A smile flitted across her lips and vanished, as though his apology briefly amused her. Later, it might amuse *him* that he still had the odd erratic, gentlemanly instinct.

"So what did you do?" she asked.

"I hit him and people I thought were my friends dragged me away and threw me on my cot where I passed out. And in the morning, I was hauled before a disciplinary hearing. The man I had hit was a superior officer. At the very least it was conduct unbecoming of an officer and a gentleman. And so I was advised to resign my commission before I was cashiered."

Her eyes widened. "Do you not have to do something very terrible for that to happen?"

He shrugged. "Many things were cast up. Occasions when I hadn't obeyed orders or had been slow to do so—some orders make no sense and only get your men killed, so I was guilty of that. Some reconnaissance mission I had led was apparently responsible for a French ambush. And I had turned back from cowardice. None of it was proved. It didn't have to be."

She had such expressive eyes that one could never get bored gazing into them. They made him think of old friendship, of comradeship and sympathy and collusion and all those other illusions he had once harboured.

"You didn't fight it," she said slowly. "It was beneath your contempt to answer such ludicrous charges, especially when your whole world was pain because your brother had died. You resigned from pique and grief and hurt that no one defended you."

"My colonel turned on me. My fellow officers turned their backs. Men who had risked their lives for me. Men I would have died for."

"They believed the lies... And when you came home, you found the rumours ahead of you, exaggerated and even viler, and your civilian friends turned their backs too."

"My family turned their backs."

"Not Bab," she said with certainty.

"Not Bab," he allowed. "My uncles, cousins, neighbours."

"One or two, perhaps. You drove the rest away as you did Bab."

"It made it easier for all of us," he managed with a casual shrug.

"But they believed in your new self, this *Snake* you portray, and that hurt even more."

"It *bored* even more." He heard the return of savagery in his own voice and strived for control. "If I stay here, I will expire from that boredom."

"And if you go away," she said, frowning in thought, "to Africa, you might find your old self again, or at least someone you can live with."

Too perceptive. But he had himself better in hand now. "I do not expect miracles, merely relief for one and all. I beg your pardon. This has been a longer farewell than I intended, when I only meant to say that you were a rare, brief, sweetness in my life, and that I wish you well."

He twisted his hand, grasping hers like a handshake. "Goodbye, Harriet Cole. Be happy."

Her fingers clung as he drew his hand free, but he would not give in. He stepped back, turned and walked to the doorway. Whatever he was turning his back on, he hadn't expected it to be so hard.

"Not like this," she whispered behind him. "My lord, not like this."

"Exactly like this," he said, lifting one hand without pausing, and swaggered out of the room. This time, he closed the door behind him and fought his way through an army of demons to his own bedchamber door.

Chapter Fifteen

Harriet gazed at the closed library door for some time. A piece of her heart seemed to be crumbling.

How had she come to care so much so quickly? She didn't know, but it had to be important and she could not give up. And yet time was running out. Tomorrow he would be gone, perhaps even at first light, as when he'd left the Duck and Spoon.

Somehow she had to change his mind before then. She wasn't even sure why. Some of it was certainly so that there was some possibility of seeing him again, but more than that, she sensed it would be bad for *him*. Through hurt and pride and sheer bloody-mindedness, he had made a mess of his life, and he could not fix that by running away.

She was sure the old Sanderly would have disdained to do such a thing and the old Sanderly was still in there. If he went now, the bitterness and self-loathing would only grow. Even if he found other satisfactions in his journeys, he would always know in his heart that he had walked away from his responsibilities as earl, his land and his people and his family.

Suddenly cold, she wound her arms around herself.

But he had told *her* the truth. Or some of it. And she was sure he had never told anyone else. Jealousy and old grudges had been at work in the army, she was sure of it. And the trivial, self-righteous gossips of the ton had done the rest. So he had made himself into what they thought he was, and instead of seeing how ridiculous they were, they had believed it. He had made a vicious circle of contempt and hatred.

When in reality there was only a good man and a lost, grieving boy beneath that haughty, sneering surface.

I need a plan. Quickly. Time to consult her troops.

First, she had to return to the ballroom, eat a bite of supper, perhaps smuggle some upstairs for her siblings who, she was sure, would be awake. Or at least Rose and Alex would be.

Twenty minutes later, she found the nursery empty. Old Nurse's snores could be heard through two doors. There was no sign of Mildred. Harriet retreated in silence and went to her own bedchamber where, as expected, she found Rose, Alex, and Orchid sitting on her bed. Lily was propped up in her own, her head resting on her hand.

"Did you wake Lily up?" Harriet demanded.

"No, I woke up myself," Lily answered, "and then they arrived. They know something."

"What do you know?" Harriet asked without huge interest. Her mind was all on Sanderly.

"It's about Lord Snake," Orchid said seriously. "He's going to fight a duel."

Harriet blinked, refocusing her eyes on her youngest sister. "A duel? Oh, no. With Lord Illsworth?"

So that was how he meant to deal with Bab's problem before he left. If he *killed* Illsworth... Her breath caught. "We have to stop him. I'll tell Mr. Martindale."

"He already knows," Alex said. "It was he we overheard talking to Sir John in the passage. Don't look like that, Harry, it's not as bad as it could be. It's only swords and ends with first blood."

But accidents happened. Wounds festered. And Sanderly didn't much care because he was leaving the country and had no real intention of coming back. What if he was the one with the festering wound?

"Swords and pistols are designed for killing," she said bleakly.

"What should we do?" Rose asked.

Harriet sank slowly onto Lily's bed. "I don't know yet. Did you discover where they are to meet?"

Alex shook his head.

"Then we have to follow them when they leave the house. It has to be at dawn. I'm sure such affairs are always at dawn."

Alex nodded sagely and they made their plan.

IT WAS NOT A GREAT plan, depending as it did merely on men's horror at conducting an affair of honour under the gaze of delicate ladies. Harriet did not really count as such, but she hoped Bab did.

In the grey half-light before dawn, two lots of two gentlemen left the house. They all carried lanterns. Illsworth and Sir John left first by the front door and strode around to the stables. The grooms must have received their orders the previous evening because it was only a couple of minutes later that, duly mounted, they rode off toward the woods.

"They're on horseback," Rose whispered from behind the rhododendron bush. "How will we catch up with them now?"

"By running and good luck," Harriet said grimly.

An instant later, Lord Sanderly and Mr. Martindale swept past in the same direction.

"Where is Alex?" Rose muttered impatiently.

"Right here," Alex said, materializing beside them. "I waited until Mr. Martindale left, then slid the note under Lady Bab's door."

Harriet set off warily, grasping Orchid by the hand. "Good. Did you hear voices? Was Bab awake?"

"I don't know."

"Well, we'd better not count on her," Harriet said. She felt guilty depriving the children of yet more sleep, but it was only once, and at least they had dissuaded Lily from trying to take part.

As soon as the riders had vanished into the trees, they increased their pace and pelted after them. And then it was surprisingly easy, for they could see a lantern winking through the trees ahead, and even make out the fresh footprints on the track. The men seemed to be in no huge rush, so perhaps there was not too far to go.

At least no one seemed to be aware yet that they were following. No one lay in wait, and when they caught the odd glimpse of Sanderly and James, they were always looking straight ahead. It was Harriet who, alarmed by odd crackles and rustlings in the wood, kept glancing over her shoulder.

Concentrate, she told herself severely.

Some ten minutes later, she made out more than one winking light ahead and they crept more carefully through the thinning trees. The greater silence made Harriet more aware than ever of every rustle in the undergrowth, every snapping twig.

And then she saw her quarries and forgot everything else.

In the dim beginnings of daylight, the duelling party had made a sort of arena of lanterns, most of which must have been transported to this spot yesterday. Harriet fumbled in her old dress pocket for the opera glasses Orchid had borrowed from Lady Grandison the day before and peered at the men in the wide arena.

There was Sir John, looking grim and disapproving beside Illsworth, who was already grasping his sword, swinging it restlessly through the air. Illsworth still looked smug, which was worrying. Shouldn't he be frightened to face a seasoned soldier? Well, he would not show it, and according to Alex, a first blood fight was not so very serious…

Sir John snatched the sword from Illsworth and marched toward the centre of the "arena", where James Martindale met him with another sword. They compared the lengths of the blades and examined each other's weapons.

At the other side of this stage, the doctor who had attended Lily was walking away from Lord Sanderly. Harriet barely noticed him. She focused on Sanderly's lean, haughty features. He seemed as bored and uninterested in the procedure as he had been with every other aspect of the party. The emotion he had betrayed last night was nowhere in evidence. He even yawned delicately behind his hand.

Harriet's heart beat faster. In the odd, upward light from the lantern next to him, his features looked sculpted and beautiful...and that was so unimportant at this moment.

Sanderly, apparently summoned by his second, strolled across the stage, unbuttoning his coat, which he shrugged off and handed to James in return for the sword. In his shirt-sleeves, he looked slight and no less elegant than before. His fingers grasped the sword with supreme casualness, like shaking hands with an old friend. He held it still by his side, with none of the theatrics of Illsworth who was again making audible passes in the air.

Sanderly is too off-hand, Harriet thought uneasily, *Illsworth too certain of his victory...*

Sir John, standing about a yard to one side and halfway between them, was addressing both combatants, holding up a bright, white handkerchief between his finger and thumb. From the motion of his hand, he seemed to be explaining that the fight could begin when he dropped the handkerchief.

The doctor and James had already cleared out of the way with the duellists' coats and hats. Sanderly and Illsworth now faced each other, only a few feet apart. They held their swords upright in front of them in a salute, Sanderly's over-casual posture and apparently loose grip seemed to say he could not really be bothered with the fuss. Harriet's stomach twisted in fear.

"Get ready," she told the children. "Remember, as fast as you can and as loud as you—"

And that was when Cousin Randolph stepped out of the trees to her left.

"Well, well," he said. "How fortunate to find you all together. One is missing, but never mind. She will come when you call."

From the field came a cry and a horrible clash and screech of steel that chilled Harriet's blood. Several shouts went up, and yet Harriet could not even look, for Randolph had snatched Orchid up like a sack of potatoes.

"Time to go home," he said coldly. "March."

ILLSWORTH WAS OVER-confident. Sanderly could see that at a glance. The man truly under-estimated his opponent, presumably believing the various rumours that Sanderly's nerve had been lost on the Peninsula, along with his honour.

All to the good. The fight would be over all the sooner.

Grandison stepped back, holding his handkerchief at arm's length, so that, even gazing at each other, both duellists could see from the corner of their eyes when it fell. Illsworth's eyes were remarkably steady, waiting... And then some small change in them, gave Sanderly a moment's warning.

Illsworth's sword slashed down and he lunged with practised speed, driving his sword straight at Sanderly's heart. His eyes blazed with triumph.

James cried out in outrage, just as the handkerchief dropped.

But it was already over.

It seemed the instinct never left. Sanderly whipped his sword downward, deflecting Illsworth's only a fraction of an instant before it would have pierced him. With a shove and a twist, he sent Illsworth's sword flying through the air. At the same time, he lashed out with one foot, sending Illsworth crashing to the ground. And then, amongst the outraged cries of the seconds and the doctor, he rested his sword point against Illsworth's wobbling throat.

"By God, you were too soon!" Grandison shouted at his man.

"You forfeit," James growled as Sanderly delicately pricked Illsworth's skin. A small bobble of blood oozed.

"And you lost," Sanderly purred. "Both the fight and your reputation, sadly."

"Nonsense," Illsworth panted. He still looked stunned by the defeat he had snatched from certain victory, but not yet afraid. "They won't tell in case there's speculation about Bab, and no one will believe *you*."

"The alternative is," Sanderly said thoughtfully, "I simply lean a little too hard *here*..."

At last, fear ignited in Illsworth's eyes.

"It's his right, isn't it?" James said to Grandison. "Your man cheated."

Grandison shrugged and curled his lips. "He did and he is no long—"

A child's scream rent the air, and Sanderly's head snapped up toward the woods where the blood-chilling sound had come from.

Orchid.

He leapt over Illsworth and raced toward the wood, even as several other voices joined the screaming. It was a fearful racket, terrifying him. Had someone stepped into one of those vicious mantraps set for poachers? Harriet's voice soared over all the rest, and the knowledge that she would never scream except as a last, very necessary resort, made his heart almost explode with fear.

He burst through the trees and the screaming turned off like a tap.

He took in the situation at a glance. He had often had to, in his soldiering days. Harriet, mercifully unharmed, stood in front of Rose and Alex, only inches away from a strange man who held the wriggling, kicking Orchid over his shoulder.

In spite of everything, Harriet smiled at Sanderly, gratitude, relief and total trust shining in her eyes. His heart broke into pieces. His head kept working.

They had all been yelling, he guessed, to confuse the man who held Orchid, as well as to attract help. Clearly, the man would not leave without the others, too.

Cousin Randolph.

Instead of drumming with her fists on her cousin's shoulders, Orchid stretched both arms to Sanderly. "Snake!"

With his sword hilt, Sanderly issued a smart smack to Randolph's head. Randolph clutched his head with a startled cry and loosened his hold. Sanderly snatched the child and stepped back.

"We came to rescue you!" Orchid crowed, her little arms hugging around his neck. "And you've rescued us instead!"

Just for an instant, his gaze met Harriet's and held.

"What is the meaning of this?" Randolph blustered. "Unhand my ward immediately, sir, or face the full consequences of the law!"

He had whirled around as he spoke, taking in Sanderly's deshabille and the sword grasped still in his free hand. His eyes widened impossibly. Both hands fell to his sides.

"Footpads!" he yelped.

"Nonsense," Harriet said briskly, marching up to take her sister from Sanderly, thus leaving both his arms free. "My lord, allow me to present my cousin, Mr. Randolph Cole. Randolph, the Earl of Sanderly."

Randolph's face began to blanch at the title, before, no doubt, everything associated with the name trickled into his brain.

"He's been fighting a duel," Alex goaded. "And you're next. Did you beat him, sir?"

"Yes, of course," Sanderly said, his mind racing on to other things entirely. Other people were blundering through the trees now to join them—the rest of the duelling party.

"Come, children," Randolph commanded. "I shall not have you associating with such a man."

"Sadly, you have no say in the matter," Sanderly drawled. It was a stab in the dark, but the only thing that made sense of Randolph's behaviour. "The entail gave you the late Mr. Cole's property, but his will never placed his children under your guardianship. Nor their inheritance under your control. The solicitors are already looking into your pilfering."

"You insult me, sir!"

"Always happy to oblige. I expect you thought to marry Harriet, too, once her spirit was broken, in order to have what was left of her fortune under your direct control."

Randolph pulled himself up to his full height. "I might have known someone like you was responsible for enticing these vulnerable young people from the safety of their home! Harriet is my betrothed bride!"

"Yes, she clearly can't bear to be apart from you," Sanderly observed.

The children giggled.

Sir John Grandison, who had been gazing around the scene in astonishment, said abruptly, "We are not acquainted, sir."

"He's our cousin Randolph," Rose said with distaste, before anyone else could answer. "Orchid really did see him at the inn yesterday, but he didn't see us. He must have heard about us, though. I think he meant to snatch us from the house before anyone else was awake, only we were on our way to stop the duel and he followed us. He grabbed Orchid and threatened to hurt her if we didn't all go with him."

"Oh, did he?" Sanderly uttered, fiercely glad of the ugliness he heard in his own soft voice. He took a step nearer Randolph who stumbled back in alarm.

Grandison's hand descended briefly, warningly, on Sanderly's shoulder. "I think, Mr. Cole, you owe me an explanation, one, preferably, that justifies your trespass. The crimes of threat, theft, and abduction should no doubt be left to the law."

"Aren't you the magistrate?" asked Alex.

"Yes," said Sir John in a satisfied manner that made Sanderly's lips twitch.

A hand slipped into his, too large to be Orchid's. Stunned, he could not look at Harriet, but her warmth seeped through him, soothing his recent fear, melting the protective ice he had fought so hard to build.

She had brought her siblings to save him somehow.

And he had known from the instant of that first scream, that he would give his life to save not only her but all the Coles.

Except Randolph.

"Where is Illsworth?" he said suddenly.

"Bolted," said the doctor bitterly. "In my carriage."

"Dash it," James said, scowling. "He has not signed our document!"

"He doesn't need to now," Sanderly said. "His behaviour in the duel saw to that. He is ruined and he knows it. Nothing he says will be believed, and if he is by chance invited anywhere, he'll know better than to accept."

Harriet's gaze burned into his face. Grandison and James and the doctor all looked at him, too. He had, after all, more cause than most to know how rumour and ruin worked.

"James!" gasped a woman's voice.

Lady Bab hurled herself from a chestnut mare, whom no one had noticed approaching along the soft track, and ran straight into her husband's arms.

"I shall be sick," Sanderly warned. "May we return to the house, Grandison, before my sister is discovered by anyone else to be quite so unfashionable?"

Harriet let out a breath of laughter.

"I still await Mr. Cole's explanation."

"There is nothing to explain, sir," Randolph said superbly. "Merely to apologize for the behaviour of my betrothed and my other wards who have taken shameful advantage of your hospitality. Harriet is playing some trick on me to gain my attention."

"I'm not betrothed to you," Harriet said instantly. "I would not agree to marry you if you were the last man on earth."

"That is certainly clear enough," Sir John murmured. "And so to your presence on my land, Mr. Cole?"

"I was calling upon you, sir."

"At dawn?" Lady Bab said incredulously.

Randolph glared at her. "I was worried! I needed to know where my cousins were! And then I saw them sneaking out of the house and behaving most suspiciously. Naturally, I followed them for their own safety. And since I discover them in such company as Lord Sanderly's—"

"His lordship is my guest," Grandison said coldly, which took Sanderly by surprise.

Randolph blinked rapidly, but only bowed by way of apology before crashing on, "I shall take my cousins off your hands forthwith. Harriet, no more of this. My carriage awaits at Grand Court." He seemed suddenly to see that Harriet's hand was in Sanderly's, for his face flushed with outrage. "Unhand my betrothed, sir, this instant."

"She is not your betrothed," Sanderly snapped. "She is mine."

Dear God, what have I said? What have I done?

"Really?" Rose cried with inexplicable delight.

Everyone else was staring at him in shock. But although he did not grip Harriet's hand, she did not let his go, only gazed up at him, and he could not look, could not bear to see…what? Outrage? Indignation? Panic? Fear? Disgust?

Reluctantly, as though a thread pulled at him in the silence, he turned his head. A tremulous smile lurked on her lips and in her bright, sparkling eyes. *She is mine…*

"I am yours," she whispered.

The surge of reasonless joy almost floored him.

"I expect you have a special license," Harriet said.

"I expect I do," he said obediently.

Even if he had tried, there had been no time to obtain such a thing, but that did not appear to strike Randolph or anyone else.

"I withhold my consent!" Randolph cried.

"You can't," Sanderly said. "Even if you have any legal rights, which I doubt, you won't risk exerting them for fear of what illegalities my people will find."

"Well, that would appear to be that," Grandison said in conclusion. "I suggest we repair to the house all together and on foot, where we shall enjoy a good breakfast and a stiff drink. And Mr. Cole may return to his carriage. You'll forgive my lack of hospitality, sir, but with my solicitors acting in conjunction with the late Mr. Cole's against you, you will agree that it would not be right. My servants will bring back the horses."

Chapter Sixteen

Harriet felt slightly numb, no doubt with the speed of events, and curiously lost without Sanderly's hand in hers. Even though she could still see him. The men walked together, making sure Randolph was surrounded. Her cousin would have to resort to the law now to get them back in his house and she doubted he would do that. Sanderly was right. He had always been up to more than penny pinching and petty cruelty.

Lady Bab walked beside her, eventually taking her arm, probably to get her attention since it was quite possible Harriet had not heard her speak.

"You are really going to marry Snake?" Bab said. "You could have knocked me down with a feather! But truly, it sounds an excellent thing, and you won't let him go to Africa, will you?"

"I...I don't know. I think he said it to spike Randolph's guns, but I don't... You got my note then? I'm sorry, I couldn't risk waking you earlier in case Mr. Martindale was with you."

"I did get it, and flew straight here after bullying poor Lady G. into telling me where the duel was to be held. Sadly, I could not be the witness you sought, but I don't really understand anything! What on earth happened at the duel?"

"I don't know either. I was distracted at just the wrong moment, when Randolph snatched Orchid. But it seemed to be over very quickly. We all yelled for attention—which, in fact, is what we intended to do anyway to nip the duel in the bud. Anyway, apparently Illsworth, who lost, took the opportunity to bolt. Lord Sanderly seems to think he is ruined and will not trouble you again."

"He was more likely to trouble you. It was your fortune he could get his grubby hands on. Or thought he could. How delicious that you were betrothed to Snake all along. I must write and tell Illsworth..."

"Don't," Harriet said urgently. "Lord Sanderly didn't mean it."

Bab's face fell. "Then he's still going to Africa?"

Harriet was saved from answering by the children who were playing all around them, running back and forth with almost delirious happiness that Randolph had been routed and that Harriet was to marry "Lord Snake."

By the time they arrived at Grand Court, Randolph had already been bundled into his carriage.

"And don't stop within ten miles," Sanderly told the coachman, who was Randolph's own servant, not one of her father's. "Or the law will take you both up. Understood?"

The coach moved forward with the children jumping up and down beside it, until Harriet called them off and swept them into the house. Suddenly, she was afraid to face Sanderly, afraid of her own emotions.

She had told him publicly that she was his, and she was in any way that mattered. But what if that appalled him, disgusted him, when he was only trying to be a friend and ensure her safety from Randolph...

"Harriet." His voice stayed her when she was halfway toward the stairs. She turned slowly to meet him. A footman by the front door stared woodenly into space. "Perhaps here?" He indicated the small salon where she and the children had first awaited Lady Grandison.

She swallowed and addressed the children. "Go up to Lily and if she's awake, tell her all. Otherwise, go straight to the nursery."

"Very well!" said Rose happily and they were soon racing each other to the top of the stairs with Orchid objecting vociferously to being left behind.

Her heart beating like a drum, Harriet walked toward Sanderly.

He opened the door of the small salon and stood aside for her to precede him. She had just stepped over the threshold when Bab and James breezed in from the front door.

"Oh, Snake, I've just realized!" she exclaimed, quite careless of the footman's presence. "Now that you've frightened Illsworth off—which is an excellent thing, of course—we'll never get my pin back!"

James grasped her by the arm and marched her toward the salon. Harriet moved further in to make way. For an instant Sanderly looked as if he would walk away, then he sighed, followed them inside and closed the door.

"Illsworth doesn't have the cravat pin," James said.

"That's what Snake thinks," Bab said, "but neither of you can possibly know for sure."

"I can," James said, and took something from his pocket. Opening his fingers he revealed a gold pin with a small, winking sapphire nestled in his palm.

Bab pounced on it in delight. "Why James! Where on earth did you find it?"

James shifted uncomfortably. "In Illsworth's room. I took it during tea the day he arrived."

Bab stared at him, stunned.

Sanderly began to laugh. "Welcome to the family, dear James. You shall do well after all. Bab, he's one step ahead of you, so no more tricks. Miss Cole, perhaps the library would suit us better. Yes, definitely."

Since the married couple were kissing with enthusiasm, Harriet hastened from the room.

They walked briskly across the hall and upstairs to the gallery and along to the library. There was no sign of Sir John or the doctor or anyone else, and despite their hurry, it still left too much time for nerves to blossom and anxieties to multiply.

She all but bolted into the library, sweeping it with one cursory glance to be sure they were the only occupants, then swung around to face him.

"I know you did not mean it and you have no earthly desire to marry me," she blurted, before he had even properly closed the door. Nor did she even register that he should not have done so at all while alone with an unmarried young lady. "Of course you know that I shall not hold you to it."

He leaned his back against the door, regarding her from eyes that were not remotely bored or sleepy, but on the contrary, glittered in a way that caught at her breath.

"You don't need to. You said you were mine."

Heat rushed into her face. "I said I was your betrothed. We can break it later."

"Do you want to?"

"I would die rather than force you to—"

"No one forces me to anything," Sanderly said, pacing slowly toward her. "You like me. You don't care two hoots about my reputation. The question is, could you love me? And if the answer to that is *no*, then run. Now."

Harriet's legs did not seem capable of holding her up, let alone running. She clutched the nearest table to steady herself.

"That is not the question at all," she said shakily. "It's whether or not you could love—"

The rest was lost as he snaked an arm around her waist, pulled her hard against him and kissed her.

It went on a long, long time, until only he was holding her up and she was utterly lost in a sea of delight and awakening desires.

"God help us both, it is simple," he whispered against her lips. "I love you now and always will."

"You cannot know—"

"I can," he said, and kissed her again, even more deeply, as though to be sure she understood. "Are you truly mine?"

"There are my sisters and Alex—"

"Their home will be with us, of course."

"And Randolph has probably stolen my modest inheritance."

"I don't want your damned inheritance. Though we'll let the lawyers pursue him for it."

"Will you go to Africa?"

"Not without you. There are probably better places to take you. Are you mine?"

"Oh God, yes," she said brokenly. "I have always been yours." This time it was she who kissed him, with such aching enthusiasm that she did not even hear the door open.

"Good grief!" exclaimed Lady Grandison, stopping dead and then slamming the door hastily. "Explain yourself, my lord!"

"With pleasure, ma'am," Sanderly said, his voice only a little unsteady. He might even have been blushing. "Miss Cole has just agreed to be my wife."

"Oh," Lady Grandison said, peering from him to Harriet. She turned on her heel. "Carry on, then. You have two more minutes!"

As it turned out, they had considerably more, but it was a fine beginning.

The ESCAPE Series

Escape of the Scoundrel
Escape of the Bridegroom (coming May 2025)
Escape of the Highwayman

About the Author

Mary Lancaster is a USA Today bestselling author of award winning historical romance and historical fiction. She lives in Scotland with her husband, one of three grown-up kids, and a small dog with a big personality.

Her first literary love was historical fiction, a genre which she relishes mixing up with romance and adventure in her own writing. Several of her novels feature actual historical characters as diverse as Hungarian revolutionaries, medieval English outlaws, and a family of eternally rebellious royal Scots. To say nothing of Vlad the Impaler.

More recently, she has enjoyed writing light, fun Regency romances, with occasional forays into the Victorian era. With its slight change of emphasis, *Petteril's Thief*, was her first Regency-set historical mystery.

CONNECT WITH MARY ON-line – she loves to hear from readers:

Email Mary: Mary@MaryLancaster.com
Website: http://www.MaryLancaster.com
Newsletter sign-up: https://marylancaster.com/newsletter/
Facebook: https://www.facebook.com/mary.lancaster.1656
Facebook Author Page: https://www.facebook.com/MaryLancasterNovelist/
Twitter: @MaryLancNovels https://twitter.com/MaryLancNovels
Bookbub: https://www.bookbub.com/profile/mary-lancaster

Printed in Dunstable, United Kingdom